WANTED: A SUPERHERO TO SAVE THE WORLD

WANTED: A SUPERHERO TO SAVE THE WORLD

BRYAN DAVIS

BOOKS BY BRYAN DAVIS

The Reapers Trilogy

Reapers

Beyond the Gateway

Reaper Reborn

Time Echoes Trilogy

Time Echoes

Interfinity

Fatal Convergence

Dragons in our Midst

Raising Dragons

The Candlestone

Circles of Seven

Tears of a Dragon

Oracles of Fire

Eye of the Oracle

Enoch's Ghost

Last of the Nephilim

The Bones of Makaidos

Children of the Bard

Song of the Ovulum

From the Mouth of Elijah

The Seventh Door

Omega Dragon

Dragons of Starlight

Starlighter

Warrior

Diviner

Liberator

Tales of Starlight

Masters & Slayers

Third Starlighter

Exodus Rising

Standalone Novel

I Know Why the Angels Dance

To learn more about Bryan's books, go to www.daviscrossing.com

Facebook - facebook.com/BryanDavis.Fans

Wanted: A Superhero to Save the World

Published by Scrub Jay Journeys
P. O. Box 512
Middleton, TN 38052
www.scrubjayjourneys.com
email: info@scrubjayjourneys.com

ISBN Print: 978-1-946253-37-8
ISBN Epub: 978-1-946253-36-1
ISBN Mobi: 978-1-946253-35-4

First Printing – September 2017

Printed in the U.S.A.

Library of Congress Control Number: 2017910659

CHAPTER 1

How Can You Have a Secret Identity When You Share a Bedroom with Your Sister?

I sat at my desk chair and aimed the grocery-store checkout scanner at my forehead, hoping the trigger's noise wouldn't wake my sister.

I glanced at her, asleep in bed. When it's time for school, she can sleep through an atomic blast, but let me try to sneak ice cream at midnight, and she shows up in her padded Tigger slippers with a big spoon in her hand. I swear those slippers turn her into a Ninja.

Taking a deep breath, I pulled the trigger. A bright light flashed for a split second, and a soft beep sounded twice.

I turned the scanner around and read its tiny screen. *Edward (Eddie) Hertz. Male. 12 years old. Caucasian. Brown Hair. Brown Eyes. Last reported height – 4 feet, 7 inches. Last reported weight – 75 pounds.*

I frowned. Still a shrimp, no matter how much I exercised. That would change … if only I could get the courage to try out the super-secret invention in my closet.

At least the scanner worked perfectly. I touched my forehead. Obviously the data liquid had penetrated the cells and left an invisible marker under my skin. It might last only a few months, but, for now, it looked like another success.

The trickier step came next.

I sat gently on my sister's bed. My head bumped her toy dragon suspended by a string from the ceiling. Covered with feathers she had plucked from a bluebird that splatted against our window, the dragon carried a tiny female humanoid made out of marshmallows, toothpicks, and yarn — a fairy princess, but I could never remember the ugly thing's super-long name.

I aimed the scanner at my sister's forehead. It had taken all day to figure out how to get the data into her skin. Offering to paint her face with sparkle makeup worked like a charm.

I pulled the trigger. The scanner flashed and beeped twice. Again I read the screen. *Samantha (Sam) Hertz. Female. 8 years old. Caucasian. Brown Hair. Hazel Eyes. Last reported height – 4 feet, 2 inches. Last reported weight – 55 pounds.*

Perfect. Now if Sam were ever kidnapped, I could track the marker and identify her no matter how much a villain changed her appearance.

Smiling, I touched the *A* emblem on the front of my shirt. Archimedes, the boy superhero, had succeeded once again.

I breathed the name in a whisper. "Archimedes." I had chosen that name for several reasons. For one, he was among the greatest scientists of all time, but the main reason is simply that it was a cool Greek name, just like the name of the most amazing guy on the planet — Damocles.

I looked at a framed photo on my desk, an autographed picture of Damocles I won in an art contest. I drew a comic strip of him rescuing my mother from our burning apartment building and sent it in to join probably ten thousand drawings scrawled by other young hero worshipers.

And I won. Of course he probably didn't judge the drawings himself, and the autograph might have been stamped on the photo by an assistant. But maybe, just maybe, the assistant told Damocles the winner's name. If *Eddie Hertz* passed into his ears at some point, that was enough for me.

I looked at my wristwatch — a mega-cool one I built from a pocket watch and a digital timer. The combination gave it an old-fashioned face and a multi-mode LED numeric readout at the center.

The hands pointed to 12:10 a.m., and the digital readout agreed. Danger always lurked in the city of Nirvana, and I was late for midnight patrol. Of course, the city already had Damocles to watch over the citizens, but he couldn't be everywhere at once. They needed a backup, and I was just the kid for the job.

A cool breeze stirred the curtains of our second-floor apartment's window. Easy access to our room was a safety hazard, so I always closed the window when I went to bed or out on patrol. Streetlamps outside could take the place of a nightlight, though Sam insisted that we leave a glowing blue fairy princess light plugged into an outlet. She claimed that the fairy watched over us at night, a dumb idea, of course, but I didn't tell her so, at least not more than a couple of times.

A rattling hum drifted in from outside. Strange. It sounded like a motor of some kind but not like a car or truck engine. It slowly increased in volume as if a machine were warming up.

I laid the scanner on my desk and fastened my gadgets belt around my waist along with the attachments — two spool lines with grappling claws, a portable hologram projector, a paintball pistol, a knife in a sheath, a glass cutter, two suction cups, two coils of wire, adhesive tape, a pair of gloves, a razor-disk gun, and a laser pen.

Everything was ready, except that my solar-powered laser pen needed a charge. But how could I turn on a light without waking Sam?

I spotted the nightlight next to the desk. It wouldn't provide much juice, but it should be enough for one patrol.

Crouching, I set the pen's butt end against the bulb. As the nightlight dimmed, the red LED power meter on the pen's side slowly increased — 5%, 8%, 10%.

The bulb popped, shattering the glass. I staggered back and landed with a *whump* on Sam's bed. My head smacked the dragon and sent it swaying back and forth inches in front of my face.

"What are you doing, Eddie?" Sam squinted at me from her pillow. Remnants of sparkle paint glittered on her face.

I hid the laser pen behind my back. "Just checking on you."

"To make sure I'm asleep so you can raid the fridge?" She sat up and halted the fairy's arcing dragon ride. "We're out of ice cream and cookies. Mom says we can't afford them till next paycheck."

I brushed a sparkle from her cheek. "Can't a brother be concerned for his sister's welfare?"

"You can't fool me." One eye closed halfway. "I see a strawberry Poptart crumb on your lip. If you really cared about me, you wouldn't be sneaking those into our room."

I swiped the crumb away with my sleeve. "You're not *that* allergic to strawberries."

"Am so." She laid a hand against her forehead and put on her I'm-so-dramatic expression. "If I even breathe the vapors, I am likely to swoon."

I rolled my eyes. Mimicking Princess Queenie, her favorite cartoon superhero, was making Sam way too theatrical. Sometimes she had no clue what she was saying. "Give me a break. When Mom made strawberry shortcake last week you licked the spoon … and the bowl … and the baking tin."

"She added the strawberries later, genius. And you should talk about eating too much. You snuck food in here three nights in a row."

"Mom never said I couldn't." I shrugged. "I've been working out a lot. I get hungry at night."

"And you're wearing that weird costume." She resumed her suspicious stare. "Are you going out again?"

"Going out? What are you talking about?"

"I've seen you. Night before last and the night before that."

"What are you? Some kind of spy camera?" I got up from the bed and walked to my closet, stealthily sliding my laser pen back to my belt. Now I had to get my mask without Sam noticing. "And it's not a costume. I just modified an Alabama football jersey."

"Take me with you, at least this once, or I'm telling Mom."

I spun back and wiggled my fingers in a creepy way. "Mephisto's gang would skin you alive and eat your kidneys. He's a mass murderer."

"He's a mass murderer," she said in a mocking tone. "You made him up just to scare me."

The hum outside grew louder. I had to get out there to see what was going on. "Mephisto's real. Get your head out of your comic books and you'll hear about him. Everyone in town talks about Mephisto."

She crossed her arms in front. "I still don't believe in him."

"Right." I touched the dragon and made it sway again. "But you believe in fairy princesses."

"Because they're real. I see them in the mirror when there's a full moon, and when you try to touch them, they burst into a zillion sparkles."

"And when you try to catch them, the sparkles go right through your hand. I know. You've told me a thousand times." I pushed her down to the pillow and pulled the cover up to her chin. "There's no full moon tonight, fairy princess, so go back to sleep."

"If you don't take me with you ..." Sam slid out

of bed and marched past me toward my closet. "I'll show Mom what you're working on in there."

"No!" I leaped ahead of her and blocked the door. "My closet is off-limits. You keep quiet, and I'll get you another Princess Quirky book."

She stomped her foot. "Princess *Queenie*."

"Whatever." I reached into the closet and grabbed my mask from a shelf. At this point it didn't really matter what she saw. "I tell you what. If you prove you can keep my patrols a secret, then I'll tell you an even bigger secret when I get back."

"At least a hint now, or I won't believe you." She set a fist on her hip. I knew that stance. Stubborn. I had to throw her a bone, something harmless. But what would work?

A gunshot pierced the silence, then another, not unusual for our neighborhood, but Mom still might check on us. I had to hurry. "Listen. When I get back, I'll tell you what I'm working on in the closet. If Mom comes in, pretend to be asleep. Got it?"

Sporting a victory smile, she nodded.

"Don't get smug." I tousled her hair. Partly because I liked her. Mostly because it annoyed her. "Now give me a Princess Power Pledge."

She raised her hand. I slapped my palm against hers, and we burped at the same time. "Remember," I said, shaking a finger, "if you break the promise, your stomach will explode and all your guts will spill out. Now go to sleep."

"You got it." She dashed to her bed and slid under the covers.

Finally. As I pulled my flexible cowl mask over

my head, I imagined Mom peering out her window to look for the source of the gunshots. She would come to check on us at any moment.

I flipped a switch on my closet's inner wall. At my bed, a holographic image appeared — myself under the covers. The projector was my greatest feat to date, though the new invention in my closet would surpass it if I could get it to work.

A shudder ran down my arms. That was one contraption I hadn't dared try on myself. Sure, I wanted to be a real superhero like Damocles, but I hadn't tested my cell-manipulation ray on a human yet. It was just too dangerous.

Leaning into my closet, I looked at the switch on the rear wall — disguised as a black widow spider. All I had to do was flip it, and the ray would bathe me in energizing ion emissions … or maybe fatally scramble my brain.

I shuddered. Not yet. Maybe tomorrow.

Footsteps creaked beyond our bedroom door. I rushed to the window, climbed out, and dropped to the fire-escape landing. After closing the sash, I crouched and peeked inside.

Mom opened the door. Light poured in from the hall. Still wearing her waitress smock, she walked close to each bed, then approached the window, looking worried, as usual. Ever since Dad died, she never seemed to be as …

I shook the thought away. I had to concentrate.

Pressing my back against the brick wall, I watched her out of the corner of my eye. She gazed through the glass for a moment before locking the window. No problem. With all the gadgets on my belt, getting back inside would be a breeze.

The moment she left and closed the bedroom door, I pulled the laser pen from my belt, flicked it on, and aimed the beam at the streetlamp near the alley entrance about thirty feet away. The beam locked on the lamp's electronic eye. Two seconds later, the light blinked off and cast our alley in dim, angular shadows.

Now under the cover of darkness, I threw a line from one of the belt's spools. The claw on the end looped around the streetlamp's protruding metal arm again and again until it stopped with a clink.

I pulled on the line. Good and tight. Of course I could use the fire-escape ladder, but I never missed a chance to practice.

I leaped from the landing and swung down. When I neared the street, I pushed the detach button on the spool. The line released, and I hit the ground running.

Without slowing, I made a right turn at the alley entrance toward the sound of the mechanical hum. The streetlamp, now behind me, flashed on. I ducked into a shadow at the side of the closest building — the bank where Mom kept her money.

I craned my neck to listen. The hum seemed to be coming from inside the building. A bank robbery? If so, why all that noise? Mephisto wouldn't be so careless, and he already robbed a bank last week. Being repetitive didn't fit his pattern. Maybe this new robbery was a diversion — a stunt designed to attract the police to keep them busy while Mephisto pulled off a bigger crime — a reasonable theory, but so far the street remained deserted.

A scrap of paper drifted on a breeze and settled at my feet. I snatched it up and scanned it — a bank deposit slip. I walked to the bottom of three steps that led to the bank's entry and eyed the wide-open front door. Suspicious. Very suspicious. Real burglars would have hidden their tracks. But why would they disable the alarm and then be so careless about the obvious break-in? The pieces weren't coming together.

I jogged to the top of the steps and sneaked inside. At the lobby's far wall, a thick metal door stood open, probably the safe. The hum emanated from there, maybe a drill bit grinding through the metal of an interior door.

I hurried back to the stairs and looked up at the underside of the entryway's overhanging awning. Yes, this would be perfect. Working quickly, I withdrew a pair of wire coils from my belt, reeled them out a few feet, added adhesive tape to the two ends, and threw them upward. They stuck to the awning. Now two wires dangled, one at each side of the stairs. With the push of a button at the wires' bottom ends, I activated a stun field between the two lines.

The field gave off a slight buzz. Not good. The robbers might hear it.

I withdrew the hologram projector from my belt, spun the dial, and browsed the images in the memory. A cop with a rifle? No, they would back off from him. A woman juggling bananas? No, that would be stupid. A bag of money? Perfect. Just the bait I needed to make them ignore the noise and face plant right into unconsciousness.

I jumped to the side of the stairs, backed into a shadow, and pointed the hologram projector at the bottom step. When I pushed the button, a fabric bag appeared, the size of a big pumpkin. Hundred dollar bills stuck out through a drawstring at the top. Now I just had to wait.

Across the street, a human form prowled along the rooftop of a three-story building. Mephisto? I shook my head. Not his style. Tunneling with a magna-gopher? Yes. Bulldozing with an octopus tank? Definitely. But sneaking across a roof? Alone? No way.

The form dashed briefly through a light, revealing an unmistakable cowl mask — black and gray, covering his face except for his eyes, nose, and mouth — just like mine.

I swallowed through a tight throat. *Damocles?*

CHAPTER 2

How Can a Kid Save a Superhero?

I couldn't believe it. The greatest hero in the world had come to my neighborhood. But if the robbery was just a diversion, he shouldn't be here. He needed to go to the scene of the bigger crime where Mephisto would be. I could take care of whatever his minions were up to. And Mephisto's scheme wasn't the only problem. If Damocles were to accidentally walk into my force field, it would zap him, and the crooks might get away.

An alarm wailed. Gunfire rang out somewhere inside the bank. Damocles threw a swing line that whipped around a flagpole protruding from the bank's overhang in front of the stairway.

With the grace of a falcon, he swooped down, released the line, and landed at the bottom of the stairs. He didn't even have to run out his momentum to keep from falling.

Dressed in army camo pants and a black form-fitting jersey emblazoned with a reddish *D*, all held in place by a loaded gadgets belt, he looked even more powerful than he did on TV, certainly more realistic and practical than the comic-book characters in their silly spandex outfits.

I stepped forward to warn him about the energy field, but he cocked his head and stared at the money bag, then the wires. I should have guessed he would notice the buzzing noise. With his hypersensitive ears, he could pick up the flap of butterfly wings.

He swiped his foot through the money bag. I turned off the hologram, making it disappear. When he looked my way, I crouched in the darkest part of the shadow. Could he see me with his super vision?

Damocles leaned over and turned off the two coils. I straightened and slid the hologram gun into my belt. Damocles could handle this. No way was I going to play the role of the kid-hero wannabe who interferes with the real hero. Still, I could watch and make a video recording.

I leaned closer to get a look at his belt. Yes, the famed Mastix hung in a translucent sheath, just like in the Internet videos. I shivered. Seeing it in person was a dream come true. But to witness the weapon in action? That would be as cool as having dinner with Albert Einstein and Batman at the same time.

Damocles pulled Mastix from its sheath and whipped it forward. Seven shining ropes lashed out and popped like rifle shots. Sparks sprayed from the knotted ends and sizzled on the steps, adding to a sizzle that the seven thongs made as they dangled from the handle and pulsed with energy.

I had to smile at the display, though I couldn't shake the idea that this robbery was a distraction or maybe a trap.

But who could trap Damocles? The legends told of an invisible shield device he wore. The shield hid the fact that he wasn't bullet proof like the cartoon heroes. But no one, not even Mephisto, had been able to get past that shield.

Another shot rang out. Damocles whipped Mastix up. A bullet slapped one of the thongs and stuck there. More bullets zinged in. With lightning-fast moves, Damocles caught them all in the thongs and slung them down. The bullets thudded on the concrete, now useless chunks of lead.

"Throw out your weapons," Damocles called with a thunderous voice as he climbed the stairs. "Surrender or feel the sting of Mastix."

A handgun flew through the doorway and clattered down the steps, then another. A man inside called, "We're coming."

In my mind, I shouted, *That was too easy, Damocles, watch out for a trap!* But I should have known he would be suspicious. He began glancing all around, Mastix gripped tightly. He then stared at the thongs. They were dark, as if the bullets had somehow drained their power. Might they have been made of a material other than lead, a substance that could absorb energy?

A thick metallic net dropped from above and fell over him. Sparks flew across his body. He rolled down the steps, making the net wrap tightly. As he writhed on the sidewalk, electricity arced across his face and shot from his ears and mouth.

Two men bolted out of the bank and down the stairs. One stopped next to the net, aimed a gun at Damocles, and pulled the trigger, but only a hollow pop sounded. A shimmering white pellet shot from the barrel and thumped into Damocles's neck. He grimaced but stayed quiet.

The men jumped into a nearby sports car. Just as the engine revved, I detached my paintball pistol and fired at the car three times. One ball missed, but the other two splashed against a rear fender, painting it red and blue. Then the car squealed away.

I slid the gun back to my belt, ran to Damocles, and touched the net. I snapped my hand back. What a jolt!

"Get away, k … kid." Damocles groaned and twitched. "You might get hurt."

"But you'll die." I whipped the laser pen from my belt, turned it on, and touched it to the edge of the net. Instantly, the pen began absorbing the electricity and shooting a beam out the other side. As soon as the network dimmed, Damocles exhaled and lay motionless, Mastix still in his grip.

I drew my shirt sleeves over my hands, grabbed the net, and walked backwards. Damocles rolled as the net pulled away. Although the weight of his muscular body made the task difficult, pushing with my legs gave me enough power to keep going.

Seconds later, the net jerked free. After tossing it aside, I knelt next to Damocles and grasped his wrist. A pulse thumped, fast and erratic.

He sucked in a breath and blinked at me. "Thanks, kid." His words came out low and slurred. "What's your name?"

"Archimedes."

"I've seen you around." He cocked his head. "Kind of an unusual name."

"Well, it's my street identity — Greek, like yours. I have to keep my real name a secret to protect my family." I touched my cowl mask. "That's why I wear this disguise."

"Trust me. I understand." Damocles grimaced again. "That shock shouldn't be affecting me so severely. I've had worse."

"One of those men shot you with something, like a shining white pellet."

"And it penetrated?"

I nodded. "In your neck."

He struggled to a sitting position and looked at his chest. "Can you see the color of the letter D on my uniform?"

I squinted. The streetlamp provided only a little light. "Kind of dark. Black or maybe dark blue."

"Not red?"

"Definitely not red."

He stared forward with a dazed expression. "And now I have nausea, a splitting headache, mild hallucinations, and the scent of strawberries in my nostrils."

"Sorry. The strawberries are from a Poptart I ate a little while ago." I glanced around. Still no one in sight. "What kind of hallucinations?"

He massaged the pellet's entry point at his neck. "Mephisto. I see his face, like a hologram." He waved Mastix around as if trying to swat a fly. The thongs stayed dull and lifeless. "A mirage. Probably hypnotically induced."

"What does it all mean?"

"I don't know yet." He struggled to his feet. "Something sinister, I'm sure."

The rumble of an engine approached. A block away, a sports car turned onto the street and drove slowly by. Paint splotched a rear fender. "That's them," I whispered. "The bank robbers."

Damocles raised Mastix and glared at them. Tires squealed. The car skidded in reverse, spun a 180, and sped away. The odor of burning rubber drifted past.

I wrinkled my nose. "Why would they come back to the scene of the crime?"

"To make sure they did the job." Damocles's eyelids twitched. "They're checking to see if they succeeded in killing me. Mephisto won't be pleased."

I breathed a whispered, "They're really part of Mephisto's gang?"

"No doubt. They probably —" He arched his back. "Argh."

"What's wrong?"

"Spasms." A new grimace twisted his face. "Something is affecting my nervous system."

"That pellet?"

"Probably a poisoned capsule." He struggled to speak. "That net must have sent a … counter-energy wave that removed my … invulnerability shield."

I nodded. "That must be why the capsule could penetrate your skin."

"I have to get … out of sight … in case they come back." He staggered toward my alley.

I hurried alongside, a hand extended to steady him if needed. "Is there anything I can do?"

"Just watch for that car." Damocles ducked into

the alley and stumbled into a garbage can, making it clatter against another. The noise scared a rat and sent it skittering into the shadows.

Damocles sat against a brick wall, took a deep breath, and let his body relax. "The hypnotic vision means that Mephisto invented a new weapon. Leave it to him to stamp his evil deed with his own image."

I crouched in front of him. "Should I do anything? Maybe call for help?"

Damocles stared at me with tortured eyes. "Too dangerous. With those villains lurking, you'd better stay hidden. Besides, there's likely no antidote. The poison will either kill me or I'll have to wait here till it runs its course."

"I can stand guard." I nodded briskly. "That's what I'll do. I'll make sure no one comes here till the poison wears off."

"Thanks." He patted my shoulder with a weak hand. "What's your real name? You can trust me."

"Hertz."

"Oh, sorry." He drew back his hand. "Sometimes I don't know my own strength."

"No. I mean my name is Hertz. Eddie Hertz."

"I've heard that name." He narrowed his eyes. "The art contest winner. You drew the comic strip about me rescuing a woman."

My heart thumped. I swallowed hard and smiled. "Yeah, that was mine."

"Who was the woman? Your mom?"

I nodded. "She's a fan of yours, too."

"It was really good artwork, especially the burning building. Lifelike. I could almost feel the texture of the craggy bricks and the warmth from the spiking orange flames."

"I just used our building as a model." I gestured with my head toward my apartment window. "I live up there with my mom and sister."

His eyes drifted that direction. "No dad?"

I shook my head. "Car accident. A little over three years ago."

"Sorry to hear that, Eddie." His face suddenly tightened again.

I cringed with him. "It's not getting better?"

"It's worse. Much worse." His respiration quickened. "I saw your hologram. Can you project anything that's digitized for three dimensional display?"

I squared my shoulders. "Definitely. I invented it myself."

"So you're the genius type?"

"Well, I guess you could say —"

"This is no time to be humble." His face twisted tighter than ever. "Still want to help me?"

"Sure. Anything. Name it."

"Take my belt off."

"No problem." I unbuckled his belt and slid it and the attached gadgets to the side. I also took Mastix from his hand and laid it with the belt. "Can you breathe better now?"

"That's not the point. I need you to hide everything from Mephisto." His voice lowered to a gasping whisper. "We can't let him know that he … he finally won."

"Won?" My heart thumped harder. "What do you mean?"

"He will go on a crime rampage if he finds out that I died."

"Died?" I shook my head hard. "Damocles, you can't die because ... because ... you're Damocles!"

"I'm sinking fast." He licked his lips. "Find a syringe in a plastic container in my belt."

I spun to the belt and reeled it through my hands until my fingers touched a plastic pouch. I popped the lid off and withdrew a syringe filled with glowing purple liquid. "What is it?" I asked as I laid it in his hand.

"I call it ... my last-chance solution." He injected the stuff into his thigh right through his camo pants. When he pulled the needle out, he exhaled. "It'll either save me or kill me." He offered a tortured smile and a wink. "We can't let Mephisto's poison do me in, can we?"

"No. Definitely not." A tear crept to my eye. "How long does it take to work?"

"Less than a minute. Then we'll know my fate."

CHAPTER 3

In Storybooks, Villains Don't Win, Do They?

My heart thumped crazily again. Waiting for this last-chance solution to work was pure torture. As the seconds ticked away, Damocles kept his eyes closed. He groaned at times, but quickly bit his lip to quiet himself. Finally, he lifted a trembling arm and pointed at his belt. "Find a red wallet in a pouch and give it to me."

I searched the belt again. After a few seconds, I found a leathery red wallet with a black button on one side and pulled it out. "What is it?" I asked as I handed it to him.

"My death switch." His hands shaking, he pushed the button and spoke into the wallet. "Damocles. Request activation. Password nine, alpha, skunk tongue, fever blisters, I love cabbage-flavored ice cream."

A computer-like voice responded. "Voice pattern recognized. Password confirmed. Contents unlocked and activated. Termination will begin in sixty seconds … fifty-nine … fifty-eight …"

"I don't really like cabbage ice cream," Damocles said as he kept his stare on the wallet. "It's just something I thought no one would guess." As the countdown continued, he opened the wallet's money pocket and poured out a silver computer flash drive. "The computer activated this, so it should work. Just run the program on the drive and you'll learn what to do."

"Forty … thirty-nine … thirty-eight …"

I stared at the drive as it lay on the ground. "Why are you trusting me with this?"

"It's too late to find someone else." Damocles grasped my wrist. "The main thing is to keep Mephisto thinking that I'm still alive. The stuff on the drive will help you. Ignore the AI unit's attitude. It will improve if you succeed."

"Twenty-five … twenty-four … twenty-three …"

"Succeed?" Kneeling, I picked up the drive and slid it into my pocket. "How do you know I can do it? I'm just a kid."

"I know. I wasn't planning to turn this over to someone so young, but time's running out. You're my only choice." His back arched, and he let out a low groan. "Besides … I've been … watching the kid with the cowl mask … who foiled several criminals." He exhaled as he finished with, "I know you can do whatever … you set your mind to."

"Twelve … eleven … ten …"

"But … but …"

"Don't worry, Eddie. Mephisto didn't kill me." Damocles peeled off his cowl. Dreadlocks spilled out over his dark skin. He pushed the mask into my hand, closed his eyes, and held the wallet against his chest. Then his head drooped to the side.

My whole body shook. I felt his wrist. No pulse.

"Five … four … three …"

I set my hand over his mouth. No breathing.

"Two … one … zero. Termination commencing." Sparks sprayed from the wallet and spewed between Damocles's fingers.

I rose and shuffled back. My throat closed. I couldn't even whisper.

The sparks crawled across his body and spread out in a widening circle, like a prairie fire consuming dry grass. As they inched along, they left nothing behind — no clothes, no skin, no bones. Thin smoke rose and drifted into the dark sky.

In less than a minute, Damocles was gone. Only the red wallet remained.

I stuffed the cowl mask under my shirt, picked up the wallet, and wobbled in place. Damocles dead? Disintegrated? How could this be?

Staring blankly, I pushed the wallet into its pouch, then picked up Damocles's belt with one hand and Mastix with the other. They seemed heavy, useless. The hero who wore this belt and wielded this whip had died. What could I do but go home and figure out the secret behind the flash drive?

The sound of the sports car's engine returned. I flattened my body against the wall. After the robbers passed, I sneaked to the alley opening and looked around. If any villains witnessed the tragedy, Mephisto would hear about it soon. He was the ringleader of filthy rats, and they all flocked to him like flies to dead fish.

"Psst. Hey, kid."

I spun toward the voice. Deep in the alley, a

human-shaped shadow waved a hand. "C'mere. I wanna talk to you."

I backpedaled into the lighted area and searched for escape routes. Normally I could outrun just about anyone, but not while carrying all this stuff.

A fire escape loomed about ten feet inside the alley. If all else failed, I could throw a line to the ladder, reel myself up to it, and then swing to my apartment's platform on the other side, but then this potential villain would see where I live.

"You heard me, kid. I said c'mere."

I slid Mastix behind my waistband. "Talking to strangers in a dark alley? That's like a nine-point-two on the mother-earthquake scale."

"I'm no stranger." A man stepped out of the alley. Tall, thin, and wearing a fedora and a loose three-piece suit, he looked like he had just walked out of an old gangster movie. He spread his arms and hands. No obvious weapon. "Don't you remember me, kid?"

"Maybe from a nightmare."

"I'm Milligan, the neighborhood, shall we say, cash-service provider. People bring me cool stuff. I turn it into cash."

I glanced at the street. Still clear. "So you're a stolen-property fencer."

"A common misconception. I cash in goods at the finest legal establishments in town."

I touched the razor-disk pistol attached to my belt. After lots of practice with plastic disks, I could hit a fly in mid-flight, but now that it was loaded with sharp razors, I couldn't use it unless a life was in danger. "If your business is legal, why are you slithering around here in the middle of the night?"

"I'm always on call. I was just doing a deal for one of the locals and came down the fire escape to, you know, keep the transaction private for my client. Then lo and behold, I see a kid holding some excellent looking merchandise. Then I figured out who he is." He took a step closer and nodded at the belt in my hand. "Eddie, I can turn your gadgets into money. I know your mom's strapped for cash. Can't even pay the rent. I can help you out. "

I gulped. He knew me. But I couldn't trust him. He looked too shifty. I wrapped Damocles's belt just below my own and buckled it in place. With my hands now free, I pulled line from the second spool on my belt and threw the claw toward the ladder above. It looped around a high rung and held fast.

Milligan took a step closer. I pushed the autoreel button and shot upward. When I planted my feet on a rung and began unfastening the claw, I stared down at him. Now what? Climb to the roof? Probably the best option. Just lie low and wait for him to leave.

He shook a finger at me. "Not helping your mom isn't smart, Eddie. And it hurts me that you're not being nice to an old family friend." He laughed. "Get it? Hurts? Eddie Hertz?"

Although I trembled, I forced a confident tone. "As if I haven't heard that stupid joke before."

Milligan let out a tsking sound. "Like father, like son. A do-gooder who thinks he's too high and mighty to work with someone like me. If you don't watch out, you'll meet the same fate. Trust me. I know what happens to people who don't play the game." He laughed with a snake-like hiss. "Good luck staying under the police radar with that big fat A on your chest. And that mask didn't fool me, so you'd better not count on it."

I glanced at the monogram on my shirt. Now it looked like a blinking neon sign telling the world my secret identity.

He stuffed his hands into his pockets and strolled down the sidewalk. "See you around, Eddie Hertz."

The moment he turned a corner, I exhaled. Good. He was gone. But his words floated in my mind like a bad odor. He said he wanted to help Mom, but was he lying? Was he really an old family friend?

I shook my head. No time to think about that now. I shot the line again, this time across the alley to my apartment's side. I leaped and swung to the opposite ladder. Now to get to the roof.

After auto-reeling the line back to the spool, I climbed the ladder to the attached stairway, then ran up the metal stairs, padding quietly to avoid waking anyone inside. Once on the roof, I ran along its flat top to our fire escape, slinked down to our window, and stooped under it. A glow shone from inside. Strange. The nightlight had broken, so something else must have been turned on.

Slowly straightening, I rose until my eyes reached the sill. A metal fragment lay there, and the window was open an inch or two. Strange again. Mom had locked it.

I picked up the metal piece and studied it. It

looked like the locking mechanism, bent and broken. I peeked inside. Light from my closet illuminated Sam standing next to my bed as she stared at my desk.

I rose a bit more. Why would she turn my closet light on? She knew she wasn't supposed to go in there no matter what.

Just as I began lifting the sash, she ducked under the desk. The little squirt probably heard the noise and decided to hide. Well, I wasn't in the mood to play nice brother. Her shenanigans had to stop.

I pushed the window fully open. Sam shot to her feet, lifting the desk completely off the floor. "Eddie? Is that you?"

"Sam?" I climbed into the room and took my mask off. "How could you … what's going … why are you picking up the desk?"

"My Princess Queenie ball rolled under it." She set the desk down and emerged from underneath holding a blue and orange striped ball. "See?"

"But how did you … I mean … the desk is so heavy." I stared at her arms, bare from her short pajama sleeves down to her hands. They looked thicker, strong and toned. "What happened to you?"

She spoke rapid fire. "I got up because I heard something in your closet. I turned on the light and saw a spider on the wall inside. I got a shoe to squish it, but when I hit it, another light came on. It made me tingle all over, but the spider was still there, so I hit it again, then the tingly light turned off. After that, I couldn't sleep, so I opened the window to find you, but I didn't see you anywhere. Then I decided to play with my ball to keep me from being lonely, 'cause it talks."

She bounced it on the floor. A tiny voice let out a squeaking phrase, too garbled to understand. When it silenced, she grinned. "Princess Queenie says she loves me."

"But how did you pick up the desk? It must weigh a few hundred pounds."

She shrugged. "I dunno. Maybe it's not as heavy as you think."

"Not likely." I threw my mask into the closet and set Mastix on my desk. After unfastening the belts, I set them on the floor. "Flex your muscles for me."

She raised both arms and drew her fists toward her head. Her biceps swelled, not as big as those of an athletic adult male but far bigger than normal for an eight-year-old girl. That meant her muscles developed in a matter of moments. The ray from my new invention enhanced her muscular cell growth and oxygen absorption.

I sat on my bed and whispered, "My superhero generator works."

CHAPTER 4

Do Little Sisters Get All the Breaks?

Barely able to keep from shouting, I nodded at Sam. "That's good. You can relax now."

She let her arms flop to her sides. "I'm hungry. Did you bring home something to eat?"

I shook my head. "No wonder you're hungry. Your metabolism is probably a roaring furnace."

"Then let's see what's in the fridge."

I shot up from the bed. "Wait. I want to try the generator on myself."

"Whatever. Just hurry up. I could eat a horse."

"Tell your stomach to cool it for a minute." I dashed into the closet and flipped the generator switch on. The light in the ceiling panel flashed. Like Sam had said, a tingle ran across my body. After a few seconds, the built-in timer kicked in, and the light turned off.

I flipped the switch back to the off position, walked to the desk, and tried to pick up one end. Two legs lifted from the floor a couple of inches, but I couldn't get them any higher. Maybe I had to wait a little longer for my muscles to grow, or the invention's actuator needed to recharge. I could always try it again later.

I set the desk down and looked at my watch — 1:28 a.m. "Okay, Sam. Go raid the kitchen, but make it quick and be real quiet."

"Do you want anything?"

"Maybe later."

The moment Sam left, I withdrew Damocles's cowl mask from under my shirt and laid it on the desk, my heart sinking again. The only superhero in the world was dead, and I couldn't do anything to stop the fiends who killed him.

My hands trembled. My stomach felt like a tight ball of knotted ropes. But I couldn't let grief immobilize me. I had to do what Damocles asked. Nothing was more important.

I turned on my computer, retrieved the flash drive from my pocket, and pushed it into the proper slot. A program automatically started. Damocles appeared on the screen, dressed in the same outfit he was wearing only moments ago, his mask in place as well as his gadgets belt, complete with Mastix. He stood next to a table covered with beakers, test tubes, and other laboratory equipment.

A robotic voice emanated from the speakers. "Camera and microphone detected."

The camera on top of my monitor flashed on. The image of Damocles blinked. "Ah. I can see you now."

"You can?" I blinked back at him. "You're controlling the camera?"

"Yes. I am an artificial intelligence replica of Damocles. Since you activated me, I assume that I somehow met my demise."

I nodded. Leave it to Damocles to write such an

amazing artificial-intelligence program. "It's true. You died a little while ago."

Damocles squinted. "You appear to be quite young. I planned to turn this technology over to a brilliant scientist or a trained athlete, not a boy."

"I'm twelve, but I'm …" How could I say it? Call myself a genius? Maybe not. "I know a lot about technology. I built my own computer from parts I got in trade from a friend, because my mother can't afford to buy one."

Damocles cocked his head. "Do you know anything about holographic imaging?"

"Plenty. I invented my own projector. Like I told the real Damocles, I can project anything that's digitized, even myself."

"Then it looks like I chose the right person." He lifted a thumb drive from the table. "The drive I gave you will provide the ability to project a hologram of me in case you need to make it appear that I am still alive."

I touched the outside of my pocket. "He … I mean, you also gave me a red wallet. What am I supposed to do with it?"

"I have no idea. I must have left that detail out of my database for security purposes. If a villain had stolen this program, he would have no knowledge that he needs the wallet."

"Needs it? For what?"

"I don't know that either, but I can provide a clue." Damocles opened a drawer in the lab table. "Do you have Internet access?"

"Yeah, but it's pretty slow."

"No problem. This is low-bandwidth stuff." He withdrew a glowing sphere from the drawer and threw it at the screen. It splashed across the monitor and brought up a web newsfeed. "The program should now be accessing my unfinished business. Since I chose you, I must have believed you to be capable of replacing me and completing these tasks in spite of your age."

Sam walked into the room with two sandwiches, one with a big bite taken out of it. "What's this?" she asked, her voice muffled by peanut butter and jelly.

"Shhh. Just watch." I read the top line of the feed — *Filtering for Mephisto news.* The next line looked like a link to an online newspaper. I clicked on it with the mouse. A new window opened, a full-page advertisement showing a photo of a man with a narrow face, thin eyebrows, and a crew cut.

I read the text out loud. "Wanted, a superhero to save the world. I am Chet Graham, president of Quasar Nuclear Physics Laboratory in Nirvana. Mephisto has stolen a fault-destabilization device from our vault, a device that could cause devastating earthquakes anywhere on the planet. He is demanding one billion dollars in ransom.

"At the risk of causing panic, I am revealing this theft publicly in order to call upon Damocles to meet with me so we can make a plan to stop Mephisto. It has been two weeks since I first tried to contact him about this looming crisis, and I hope public pressure will force him to be the superhero most people consider him to be. Damocles, I beg you. Help me stop this catastrophe. You're the only person who can save the world."

"Wow!" Sam said as she continued chewing. "So Mephisto *is* real."

"I told you so. And I saw Damocles tonight."

Her brow lifted. "Really? Did you talk to him?"

"For a little while." I couldn't tell her that he died. That had to stay a secret for now.

Sam swallowed and licked her lips. "I wonder why he won't meet with that guy."

"I'm sure he has his reasons." I clicked back to Damocles and spoke toward the camera's built-in microphone. "Did you schedule an appointment to meet with Chet Graham?"

Sam pointed, her mouth again full. "Is that him? Is that Damocles?"

Damocles bowed his head. "Yes, I am Damocles, Miss …" He paused, prodding for a last name.

Sam swallowed her mouthful. "Hertz."

"I'm sorry to hear that. What sort of injury did you sustain?"

She giggled. "No, silly. Hertz is my name. Samantha Hertz."

"And I'm Eddie Hertz, also known as Archimedes." I leaned closer to the monitor. "I read the ad that asked you to meet with Chet Graham. Did you or did you not agree to meet with him?"

Damocles picked up a small notebook from the lab table and flipped through the pages. "I have a meeting scheduled tomorrow night at midnight with Mr. Chet Graham on the roof of the Stellar building."

"The Stellar building." I blew out a sigh. "That's downtown. I'll have to take a bus."

"*You'll* have to?" Sam asked. "Why do you have to be there?"

"Because ..." I looked her in the eye. She wouldn't rest until she learned the truth. I let my gaze shift to her bulging arms, then to my arms, still as thin as usual. Maybe I would need Sam as a backup.

During the next few minutes, I told her everything — my adventures as Archimedes, the superhero generator in the closet, the fencer in the alley, Damocles's death, and my need to replace him so Mephisto wouldn't know that he had died. I even showed her his cowl mask as proof.

She listened carefully, chewing and nodding. For a young squirt, she was really smart. She could memorize stories in just one telling.

When I finished, she flexed her bicep. "Then I should be the superhero Mr. Graham needs to stop Mephisto's plans."

"You?" I laughed under my breath. "You wouldn't last five minutes in the real world. It's dangerous out there. It's not like you're Wonder Woman. You're just a girl."

"No, I'm not Wonder Woman. My superhero name is Princess Queenie Unicorn Iris Ponyrider Buttercup Olive Lover Rosey Is Posey."

I mentally recited the name. The least I could do was memorize it and humor her. "Is it all right if I use the initials and call you Princess Quipbolrip for short?"

"No." Staring at me, she chewed on.

I rolled my eyes. "Listen. I have to go to the Stellar building alone. The fencer I told you about might come by, so you need to stay here and protect Mom. The generator hasn't worked for me yet, so you'll have to be the muscles for our superhero duo until it does."

She smirked. "So I'm Superman, and you're Wonder Woman."

"Don't get a big head. The superhero generator probably needs to recharge. By this time tomorrow, I'll be able to kick your butt."

"I'd like to see you try it." She crossed her arms and flexed, obviously enjoying the bulging muscles.

"We're not going to fight each other. We're a team." I glanced at my watch again — almost two a.m. "Let's get some sleep. We need to be wide awake for tomorrow night."

Sam stuffed the rest of the second sandwich into her mouth. She waved at the monitor and whispered in a garbled voice, "Good night, Damocles."

Damocles gave a half bow. "Good night, Miss Hertz. I hope you feel better soon."

"But I'm not —"

"Shhh." I pushed Sam toward her bed. "He's just an artificial intelligence image. He can't figure everything out."

She slid under her covers and stared up at me, her eyes wide in the dim light. "I think I'm going to like being a superhero."

I sat on her bed. "Why?"

She looked at a corner of the ceiling where a

crack ran down the plaster wall, then at her dresser and its three missing pull handles. "Maybe I could make some money with my super strength."

I lowered my voice to a whisper. "We're not all that poor. At least we have a place to live."

Her brow furrowed. "While you were gone, I heard Mom talking on the phone. She was asking someone for rent money. She sounded scared."

"Who would she call at this time of night?"

"Someone called her. I heard the phone ring."

"Did you catch the name?"

She nodded. "Milliken … or something like that."

"Milligan. He's the fencer." I squinted. "How could you hear all that?"

"Well … she was crying." Sam looked away and sniffed. "Maybe that made her louder than usual."

"Hey." With a gentle hand, I turned her head back toward me. "What's wrong?"

Her chin quivering, she locked her teary eyes on me. "Why did Daddy have to die?"

"I don't know, Sam. I just don't know." How many times had I asked that question myself? Even Mom couldn't explain why the brakes failed a day after they were inspected. And since Milligan mentioned me meeting Dad's fate, the failure seemed more suspicious than ever.

I whispered to myself, "Maybe someone murdered him."

"Murdered?" Sam blinked. "Who would murder Daddy? He was the nicest man in the world."

"Of course he was. I … I was just thinking too much." I rose from the bed, stepped back, and looked her over. She had heard my quiet whisper and Mom's phone call. What could it all mean?

I cupped my hands over my mouth and whispered as softly as possible, "Princess Queenie is a space alien."

Sam crossed her arms and scowled. "She is not! She's a fairy!"

I lowered my hands. "Well, Miss Fairy Princess, it looks like you have super hearing."

CHAPTER 5

How Can You Keep a Secret from a Sister Who Has Super Hearing?

Something bounced on my bed. "Time to get up, lazybones."

I groaned. Sam's voice. Perky. Annoying. The chirping of a songbird that needed to be strangled.

I half opened an eye. Rays of dawn peeked through our window. Since it was early July, it couldn't be later than six. "Go back to bed."

"But I'm not sleepy. And I'm hungry."

I glanced at her arms — just as pumped as before. Her metabolism was still working overtime. "Then get a bowl of cereal. And don't wake Mom up. It's Saturday. I think she has the day off."

Sam hopped off the bed and dashed out of the room, already dressed in jeans, T-shirt, and … a purple cape?

Sighing, I rolled out of bed and turned the computer on. An email message popped up — Jack from Electronics Depot.

Hey, Eddie. Got ten surplus solar cells you can have on the cheap. They'll cost you just two hours of play time with your VR helmet. But you have to unlock all the beta weapons. I want to try the atomic cannon against the glowbots. Let me know.

I closed the message. No time to barter with Jack. I plugged my hologram projector's interface cable into the computer and copied the digitized image of Damocles from the thumb drive to the projector's memory. It took longer than usual. Probably a high-resolution image.

When it finished, I dialed up the image, pointed the projector at the bedroom floor, and pressed the button. In the usual flash of light, Damocles appeared, clear and life-size, once again wearing his cowl mask and gadgets belt. Yet, he was motionless, standing at attention as if waiting for a command.

A voice came from behind me. "Does your projector have an AI processor?"

I looked back at the computer. On the screen, Damocles stood next to the lab table, a magazine spread out over his hands. He flipped a page as if casually browsing ads for mad-scientist gear.

I shook my head. "It's just a projector, like a dumb terminal."

"Then you'll have to use mine." Damocles looked up from the magazine and touched his waist. "You'll find it on my belt."

I grabbed the belt from the floor and searched the various pouches until I came across a gun-like device that resembled my own projector. I pulled it out and squeezed the trigger. It buzzed, and a flicker of light emanated. Then it sizzled and grew scalding hot. I dropped it and blew on my hand. "I think the net fried it."

Damocles nodded. "The Internet has many viruses that can cause computers to malfunction."

"Not the Internet. The electrified net that fell on you. It cooked the projector."

"Ah. Then try mine. You'll find it on my belt."

"Stupid, buggy program." I leaned closer and spoke slowly. "Listen. The hologram projector that you had on your belt is malfunctioning. I don't have access to a projector that has artificial intelligence capabilities."

"Then you will have to get a new one." Damocles flipped through the magazine and stopped on a page. He ripped it out and threw it at the screen. An Internet ad from Electronics Depot appeared showing a handheld computer that included a 360-degree camera and life-tech speakers, the exact device I had dreamed of getting for weeks.

"I saw your email," Damocles said. "So I found this ad. Make Jack an offer for it. Then you'll be able to animate the hologram."

"I don't have anything worth that much. I just trade for parts and build stuff myself."

Damocles let out an exaggerated sigh. "Then Mephisto will find out that I'm dead. He'll unleash a storm of crime on Nirvana that will destroy homes, families, and … and whatever else gets destroyed in crime storms."

"Don't try the guilt trip. I'm not gullible. I just don't have anything —"

"You have the VR helmet. Offer it to Jack, and he can atomic blast virtual-reality glowbots forever."

"But it took me two months to build that helmet. It's my main way of getting the parts I need."

"Suit yourself." Damocles rolled the magazine into a tube. "I'm dead, so Mephisto's cruel oppressions won't affect me, but you have your injured sister to consider."

"I told you to stop the guilt trip."

"It's in my programming. If guilt doesn't work, shame is next. I plan to talk about how it seems that I chose the wrong person, that I died thinking a courageous young man would step into my shoes and —"

"All right. All right. I'll make the offer." I glared at the screen. Damocles said to ignore the AI unit's attitude. The real Damocles would never be so manipulative. Anyone who remembered the details of my art entry had to have a heart of gold.

I stepped into my closet and grabbed the VR helmet from the floor. While I was in there, the black-widow switch caught my attention. The generator had been recharging for several hours. Maybe it would work on me this time. I flipped the switch up. The light flashed on. Again, tingles crawled along my skin.

When I turned the light off, I stepped out of the closet and flexed my biceps — defined and wiry, but no bigger. Time would tell if it worked.

I got dressed in jeans and a Nirvana University T-shirt, the one with the boxing pig on the front. Jack was a big fan of the Fighting Warthogs. He always worked on Saturday, and since they opened at nine, I had plenty of time to get there.

After using the bathroom, I hurried to our eat-in

kitchen. Sam sat at the three-person table on the near side, shoveling a big spoon from a huge salad bowl. "There's enough cereal for you," she said as soggy Cheerios spilled from her mouth, "but we're out of milk."

"I'm not surprised. The way you're eating, I think we'll need to rent a cow."

She swallowed her mouthful and stared at me. "Why that shirt? You going somewhere?"

"Yeah. To Electronics Depot." I looked at her arms. They were slightly smaller than before, but maybe because she was relaxing them. Still, I needed to keep an eye on her. Since Milligan seemed to be a night crawler, Mom would probably be safe this time of day. "Want to come with me?"

"Sure." She stood on her chair and leaped to the floor, making her cape billow.

I touched the purple towel's frayed edge. "You have to leave your cape here."

"But I'm a superhero now."

I firmed my lips. The best way to convince her might be to play along. "Listen, Sam. Every superhero has a secret identity. If you run around town with a cape, everyone will know that Samantha Hertz and ..." I searched my memory. That crazy name was in my brain somewhere. "Princess Queenie Unicorn Iris Ponyrider Buttercup Olive Lover Rosey Is Posey are one and the same person."

"You got it wrong."

"The superhero name? No, I'm sure you said —"

She shook her head hard. "You got it wrong.

I'm Princess Queenie Unicorn Alice Rosey Posey Buttercup Iris Tassels."

"Princess Quarpbit?"

"Stop it!" She crossed her arms tightly. "Say it right, or I'm wearing the cape to Electronics Depot."

"Okay, okay." I looked her in the eye. "You're Princess Queenie Unicorn Alice Rosey Posey Buttercup Iris Tassels."

"Perfect." She detached the cape and hung it over her chair. "Are we taking the bus?"

"I wish. We have to walk. But maybe I can squeeze some money out of Jack so we can pay for a ride home."

"And a snow cone?"

"We'll see." I combed my fingers through her unruly locks. "If you brush your hair and put a pink ribbon in it, maybe that'll help our cause."

"Goody." She skipped to the bathroom and disappeared inside.

I grabbed pen and paper and wrote a quick note for Mom. Since she worked till eleven last night, she would probably sleep past seven. No use waking her up.

With note in hand, I tiptoed to her bedroom. The door was ajar. I peeked through the gap. She lay asleep, curled on her side. Again on tiptoes, I sneaked in and laid the note on her night table. A pill bottle sat next to the lamp. Unusual. I hadn't heard her say anything about being sick.

I leaned close and read the bottle's label — Nexium. It sounded familiar. Something for ulcers, maybe? I could look it up later.

As quiet as a mute mouse wearing sneakers, I hurried out of the room and snatched my backpack from a hook on the wall near the main door. While walking around the apartment, I collected three snack bars, the VR helmet, Damocles's flash drive, and my hologram projector and stuffed them into the backpack. Then I shot off an email to Jack telling him I'd be at the store at 8:30, a half hour before it opens.

Sam joined me, her face washed and her hair neatly fastened in place with a pink hairband. Wearing a black skirt with matching leggings and a purple top, she oozed little-sister cuteness. No one would ever guess she had super powers. We scampered out of our apartment and down the stairs. That route was faster than our slow-as-a-crippled-turtle elevator.

Once on the sidewalk in front of our building, Sam slid her hand into mine. "My secret identity is Samantha Coolio, a little girl who's scared of the city streets. She is blind in one eye and has throat cancer. Her parents were killed by a swarm of rabid weasels, so now she's an orphan."

"An orphan, huh? Good idea."

Her vigorous nod shook her ponytails. "So you'll have to hold my hand, but if a bad guy jumps us, I'll transform into Princess Queenie Unicorn Esmeralda Sabrina Taryn Rosey Olive Buttercup Iris Tassels."

"So now you changed it to Princess Questrobit."

"My superhero name hasn't changed. You just keep forgetting."

"Whatever."

"Morning to ya, Eddie. Samantha."

I pivoted. Barney the maintenance man stood halfway up a ladder that leaned against our building. Although it was still morning, sweat glistened on his sunburned face. "What's up, Barney?"

"Seems that I am." Wearing a carpenter's utility belt over dirty jeans and gray t-shirt, he tromped down the rungs. "Got two windows to fix. Yours is next, but I can get to it from the fire escape."

I angled my body to see the side of the building, but the window was out of sight. "Who reported it?"

He shrugged. "Your mom, I guess. I just got a call from the landlord to fix it."

"Well, I think my mom's sleeping, so —"

"I'll be as quiet as a woodpecker on a downspout." He pulled a hammer from his belt. "Sorry, but it's part of the job."

"Are you sticking around all morning?"

"Yep. After the window, I have to set rat traps. The beasts are multiplying faster than a calculator. Caught two of them picking out baby gifts from a ratalogue." He snorted a laugh. "Get it? A ratalogue instead of a catalogue?"

"Yeah, I get it." I resisted the urge to roll my eyes. "Hey, can you kind of keep an eye out for my mom while we're gone? I think I saw a prowler near our window last night."

"You can count on me." Barney pretended to bop someone with his hammer. "Any strangers will have to get past me first. I have a black belt in six different blunt tools."

"Thanks. We'll be back in a couple of hours."

As Sam and I walked hand in hand, I glanced at her arms. Her muscles were still much bigger than normal, bulging under her sleeves.

I looked at my own arms. Normal. No sign of molecular transformation. It seemed that my generator had worked only once and then died. Maybe I could fix it if I could find the right parts, but giving up my VR helmet made that possibility look pretty dim.

We took the long way to bypass what locals called the Dead Zone — a haunt for drug dealers, black-market traders, and undead beings, though I wasn't ready to believe in the ghosts and zombies people talked about. Adults were probably just trying to keep kids away from the crime-infested area.

When we arrived at the store, I pressed my nose against the glass door and peered inside. Jack was playing a video game on a giant-screen TV. A clock on the wall said half past eight. I checked my wristwatch — 8:29 a.m. Close enough.

Still holding Samantha's hand, I tapped on the glass with a knuckle. Jack held up a finger, his stare riveted on the TV. After a few seconds, his shoulders slumped, and he laid the game controller on a chair.

As he sauntered toward the door, his gray ponytail swayed behind him. He once told me he came from the hippie generation and couldn't stand the thought of cutting his hair or shaving his beard, though he kept the beard fairly short and neat.

He unlocked the door and swung it open, grinning. "Well, well, well. It's Megahertz and his little sister Kilohertz."

"Yeah. Good one." I pushed past him, guiding Sam at my side. "I haven't heard that one ... today."

Jack touched my backpack. "Did you bring it?"

"Yep." I slid the straps down and unzipped the pack.

As I lifted the helmet out, Jack licked his lips. "I'll get the solar cells."

Just as he turned, I grabbed his arm. "Wait. I want to make a different deal."

"A different deal?" Jack rubbed his thin hands together. "What else you got?"

"First, I don't want the solar cells. I want that handheld computer you have on sale."

"The Z-ninety? Why? It's old technology. We're just draining the inventory to get some cash for the new stuff."

I hid a smile. Jack fancied himself a master negotiator, but he was really as clever as a dung beetle. He had already given me the upper hand. "Since it's not really worth much, then you'll have to throw in a power cord and a master interface plug so I can connect my hologram projector."

"Well, it still sells for a couple hundred bucks, and the adapter is fifteen, but you won't need the power cord if you don't mind using regular batteries when the rechargeables go dead. The unit takes both kinds."

"I like rechargeables. How many helmet hours is it all worth?"

"Way too many. You can't trade hours for that much dough."

"How about if I trade the helmet itself?"

Jack's mouth dropped open. His tongue nearly hung out as he splurted, "Sold."

He reached for the helmet, but I pulled it back. "Plus cash. I know this helmet's worth more than two hundred. It's one of a kind. Way more advanced than anything on the market. You know that."

"Yeah, yeah, but you're here begging for a trade, so I get to set the value." Jack looked upward for a moment, then at the helmet. "I'll add fifty bucks."

"Fifty? You gotta be kidding. I could get five hundred in the Dead Zone."

He waved a hand. "Then go to the Dead Zone. If you come out alive with the five hundred, then I'll personally pat you on the back. More than likely I'll be coming to your funeral instead."

I looked past Jack at an open door to an office. His boss sat at a desk shuffling through a stack of papers. I extended the helmet to Jack. "Tell you what. You show this to your boss, and I'll accept whatever he says it's worth. Deal?"

"Deal." He grabbed the helmet and tucked it under his arm. "No backing out."

"It goes both ways. You can't back out either."

"Of course. I'm no cheat." He marched to the office and closed the door.

I whispered to Sam, "Tell me what they say."

She locked her stare on the door. "Jack asked his boss how his wife is doing. … She's fine. Her arthritis is acting up, though. … Jack is talking about your helmet. He says they can easily get three thousand bucks for it from a research guy he knows. … His boss says great. They'll buy it. … Throw the kid a bone and offer two hundred plus the other stuff he wants. That should make him happy."

The door opened. Jack walked out with a wad of cash clutched in his fist. The helmet sat on the boss's desk. With a wide grin, Jack counted out two hundred in twenties into my hand. "I'll get the computer and cables."

"But you and your boss agreed that it's worth three thousand, not two hundred."

He blinked. "What? How could you possibly —"

"And when you go back for the rest of the money, please tell your boss that I'm sorry about his wife's arthritis. I hear it can be very painful."

Jack's face reddened. "Then you must've heard every word."

"I guess since you're no cheat, you'll get the rest of the money."

He whipped around, hurried back to the office, and closed the door.

Sam was already craning her neck to listen. Smart girl, as always.

"I just hear scratching noises."

I nodded. "They're probably writing messages."

Soon, the boss stormed out, stopped in front of us, and stared at Sam. Her smile wilted under his glare. Then he shifted his bloodshot eyes toward me. Wearing a black toupee that looked like a plastic cap sprouting monkey hair, he blurted, "I've got twelve fifty in the safe. With the computer, that adds up to fourteen fifty. Take it or leave it."

His breath smelled like coffee and cigar smoke. I

hid a swallow and tried to keep from squeaking. "I'll take it."

He cursed under his breath. "I'll tell Jack to get your stuff."

Within five minutes, Sam and I walked out of the store with the computer, the cables, and twelve hundred fifty dollars in cash.

Sam's smile stretched wide enough to break her face. "We could get a bunch of snow cones with that much money."

I stuffed the bills into my pocket. "We'll get snow cones, but a lot of this money is going to pay for our rent. That's more important."

After buying snow cones — strawberry for me and blue raspberry for Sam — we rode the bus home. When we arrived at our corner, Sam slurped the last bits of ice and dripped blue liquid down her chin. Then we walked toward our building, this time skipping the hand holding. Her sticky fingers might glue us together for good.

Along the way, I compared our arms once more. Hers were still bulky. Mine? Skinny as ropes.

I stopped at a first-floor apartment where our landlord lived — Mrs. Abercrombie, a blue-haired old spinster. And no wonder she never married. She spat tobacco juice into a plastic cup every few seconds, had teeth as brown as dog droppings, and smelled like an outhouse.

She opened the door a crack and peeked out. "Whaddaya want?" she asked with a growl.

"To pay our rent." I pulled some money from my pocket and showed it to her.

"Well, it's about time." She opened the door fully. Wearing a short white bathrobe that exposed most of her thin, hairy legs, she extended a hand.

I gave her our late rent, part of the next payment, and added an extra twenty as an apology.

"Where did you get all this cash?" she asked, one painted eyebrow lifting as she counted it. "Your mother's been begging for more time like a pathetic little lapdog."

"I sold one of my inventions."

She snorted, spilling brown juice over her bottom lip. "Don't lie to me, Eddie. You're probably stealing stuff and fencing it with Milligan."

"Look. You got your money. If you think I'm a thief, then call the cops. I'll be glad to tell them what's growing in your window planter."

"Rabble." She slammed the door in my face. I backed away a step, wishing I had the strength to kick it open.

"I don't like her," Sam said.

"No one does. Not even Mom."

"And she smells like burnt popcorn."

"Burnt popcorn?"

Sam nodded. "With butter."

I took a whiff of the air. Just the usual mildew. No popcorn. Either Sam's inferno of an appetite was making her imagine food, or she had a super-sensitive nose to go along with her other powers.

I gestured with my head. "Let's check on Mom."

CHAPTER 6

What Do You Do With a Ghost Superhero?

Sam and I hurried up the stairs. When we reached our apartment door, it opened. Mom stood at the threshold wearing a fresh waitress smock to go with pressed jeans and a black "Magruder's Italian Restaurant" polo. Her worried expression melted into a smile that did a bad job hiding her sadness. "So you two rascals went out on a shopping expedition, did you?"

I shrugged my backpack. "Yeah. Got some stuff from Jack. I traded my VR helmet."

Mom's eyes widened. "You did what?"

"And we got snow cones." Sam spread out her blue-stained hands.

"What happened to your arms?" Mom grabbed Sam's wrist and looked her over. "You're all swollen. You must have had an allergic reaction." She gave me a scolding stare. "Eddie, I've told you about her sensitivity to food dye. The snow cones were probably loaded with it."

I hid my relief at her mistake. "I didn't think about it. Sorry."

Mom pushed Sam inside. "Get in the tub and scrub every inch. Eddie will get you some Benadryl."

I slid off my backpack. "You look like you're kind of stressed out."

"Probably because I'm working two shifts today, including prep for the lunch crowd. And I'm closing, so I'll be late tonight."

"How late?"

"Around midnight, but it could be later."

I tried not to flinch. I had to leave at around eleven, and I'd have to take my hologram projector with me, so she wouldn't see my phantom clone tucked safely into bed. "Are you working so many hours because the rent's late?"

Her brow furrowed. "Who told you that?"

"You know you can't hide stuff from me." I withdrew the remaining cash from my pocket and handed her all but what I needed for bus fare and a bit extra. "I paid the overdue rent and part of next month's. This is for food."

As she stared at the money, a tear sparkled in her eye. "You sold your helmet to pay our rent?"

"More or less. I kept a little for stuff I need. I hope you don't mind."

"Mind? Mind?" She pulled me into a tight hug. "Eddie, I don't know what I'd do without you."

When she let me go, she brushed tears from her cheeks with trembling hands. "Listen. On the way home tonight, I'll stop at Fred's and get some ice cream, and we'll have sundaes for breakfast tomorrow. How's that sound?"

"Great, Mom, but since the rent's paid, can't you skip the late shift?"

She ran her fingers through my hair. "No, silly. I

promised Victor. But I can cut down my hours next week, and we'll plan an outing for the three of us. All right?"

"I guess so, but —"

"I gotta go." She scooted past me and headed for the stairs. "We can talk about it over ice cream tomorrow." As her no-slip sneakers squeaked on the steps, she called back, "And don't forget Sam's Benadryl. It's in the medicine cabinet."

Seconds later, she was gone.

I heaved a sigh. Getting out tonight without her noticing would be tough. I often avoided going on patrol whenever she planned to work late, though sometimes I would catch a nap and leave after she came home and checked on us.

Exhaustion swept over me like a ten-ton weight. I yawned. I had plenty of time to get some sleep. Better to be wide awake for testing Damocles's hologram later.

I took the new computer out of its box along with its detachable power cord and plugged the unit into the wall to charge its battery. After helping Sam get her lunch, I gobbled a baloney sandwich, put my watch on the desk, and flopped into bed.

Sleep pounced on me like a lonely puppy. I dreamed about strawberries battling blue raspberries on a field of crushed ice until something shook my bed. I grabbed the mattress and looked around. The entire room rattled. The crack in the wall widened.

Sam ran into the room, shouting, "I think it's an earthquake!"

When I reached out for her, she jumped into

bed with me. For the next twenty seconds, we hugged each other and rode out the tremors. Finally, they stopped.

"Mephisto?" Sam asked.

"Has to be. Nirvana hasn't had an earthquake in a hundred years." I jumped out of bed and flipped on my desktop computer. Nothing happened. I hit the light switch. Again, nothing. "Power's out."

I picked up my backpack and laid it on the bed. After withdrawing my hologram projector and unplugging the new handheld computer, I added the projector adapter and snapped the two units together. The combination still fit in my hand and wouldn't be too heavy attached to my belt.

I turned on the projector. When it powered up, I plugged in Damocles's flash drive and waited for it to process the loaded image. As before, the AI unit appeared in clear 3D, though still motionless.

While the computer portion of my combined device powered up, I glanced at the desk clock — dark. My watch lay next to it, just out of reach. "Any idea what time it is?"

"I was watching Princess Queenie," Sam said, "so it's between five and five-thirty. It was almost over, so probably five-thirty."

"Then I slept more than four hours. The computer battery should have enough juice." I looked at the window. Even closed, car-horn blasts passed through. "Mephisto scheduled the quake for rush hour. That's the best time to cause the most chaos."

Sam laid her hands over her ears. "People are shouting bad words."

"With all the signals out, it's probably the worst traffic jam in history." I drew a mental picture of the jam — a tangled mass of cars and trucks going nowhere. What about the buses? Would they run at all? If not, I might have to walk downtown tonight.

I booted up the handheld computer's embedded AI program. Within seconds, Damocles began moving. The built-in camera, a sphere on top of the unit, lit up with a blue glow all the way around. "Can you see us?" I asked.

Damocles nodded. "So you were able to get the devices you needed. Well done." The computer's life-tech speaker made his voice sound like he was really in the room — loud and resonating.

I gave him a rundown of the recent events as well as the problems I now faced, including getting to the Stellar building. I finished with a sigh. "Do you have any ideas?"

"My current programming provides instructions to help my successor create this hologram. Now that you've succeeded, I need to load the next programming phase — the essence engine." Damocles leaned toward me. "Do you have the red wallet?"

I picked up Damocles's belt and withdrew the wallet from its pouch. "Right here, but you said you didn't know anything about it."

"That was before this phase was triggered. Turn the wallet inside out, and you will find a standard computer interface. Plug it into your handheld unit, and I will access the code."

I opened the bi-fold wallet. On one side, the leather material covered a circular bulge about twice the size of a silver dollar, but there seemed to be no zipper to access whatever was hidden underneath.

Inserting my thumbs into the money pocket, I turned the wallet inside out and found a short cable deep inside. I plugged it into one of the handheld computer's ports. "Done."

Damocles bowed his head. "It has been a pleasure, Eddie. Stand by for further instructions."

The image flickered and faded. Then Damocles's voice emanated from the speaker. "Create a password. Make sure it cannot be guessed by anyone."

I brought up the screen's keyboard and tapped "cabbageflavoredicecream." The screen flashed, and Damocles's hologram reappeared, clearer than ever. He looked like a real person, as if he actually stood in the room with us, though this time he wore no mask. His dreadlocks framed his chiseled ebony face as he looked straight at me. "Eddie?"

"Yeah. Sam and I are still here. Did your AI brain reboot or something?"

"I'm not an AI unit." He scanned the wall behind me. "I must be inside your apartment. This looks like the room you drew in your comic strip." He pointed. "Is that the window I carried your mother through?"

"Right. In my story my mother was checking on Sam and me, and she —" I gulped. "How could you know that? We talked about my comic strip after you programmed the AI unit."

"Like I said, I'm not an AI unit." The camera in the handheld zoomed in on me, and the tiny screen displayed my puzzled expression. "When I died, the red wallet absorbed my essence, and now it's in your computer. I have all my memories, experiences, and thinking skills. The only thing I lack is my body."

My hands trembled. He was alive again ... sort of. "So you planned your death scenario, a secret way to survive if Mephisto finally figured out how to kill you."

"That explanation will do for now, though there is more to it."

"So what's the next step in your plan?"

"I am aware of what you told the AI unit, so we need to get to the Stellar building and meet with Mr. Chet Graham."

A knock sounded at the main entry door. I handed the projector/computer combination to Sam. "I'll be right back."

I hustled through the apartment and called out, "Who is it?"

"Barney. I have a message from your mom."

I unlocked the door and opened it. Barney stood in the hall, carrying a trap with a dead rat dangling from it. A hunk of cheese protruded from its mouth. "Your mom sent the restaurant's delivery guy on a bicycle to ask me to check on you." He scanned the walls and ceiling. "I don't see any new cracks here. Apartment Three-F nearly split in half. I had to move that Russian couple and their blind sheepdog to Apartment One-B. The tub faucet leaks, but that's no big deal. They never bathe."

"Thanks for letting me know." I pushed the door. "If you can get a message back to my mom, tell her Sam and I are fine."

He stopped the swinging door with a hand. "I'd better have a look at the crack in your bedroom."

Just as he took a step inside, I blocked his way. "It's all right. No worries." I nodded at the rat. "Sam has lots of allergies, so we can't let that near her."

He lifted the trap and watched the rat's body sway. "Sorry. I'll get outta here and send a message back with the delivery guy." As he walked to the hallway, he added, "And don't be surprised if your mom doesn't get back till morning. Magruder's is being set up as a shelter, so she might be serving customers all night. Not that she could take the bus home anyway. The routes are all closed. But she'll make a lot of tip money."

"Yeah. Well, we'll be fine." When Barney walked out, I began closing the door again. "Don't worry about us."

"Sure thing. I'll check on you in the morning."

I closed the door the rest of the way. After setting the deadbolt, I clenched a fist. Perfect. Since Mom would be at the restaurant all night, I could take the projector to the Stellar building, and no one would be the wiser.

I walked toward the bedroom. Of course, I'd have to take Sam with me, but that would be fine. With all the chaos on the streets, no one would pay attention to two kids sneaking downtown. But I'd have to get an early start — give Sam a big dinner and hit the road with her at dusk.

When I entered the bedroom, Sam was dancing on the bed, making her hanging dragon sway while

Damocles hummed a tune, bouncing on his toes with the rhythm. Then he broke into song.

"Princess Queenie, fairy blessed, of all the fairies, you're the best. Spread your sparkles far and wide. Take me on a sparkle ride."

When they saw me, they stopped abruptly. Damocles straightened and smiled. "Your sister is an excellent dancer, but she says you won't sing with her."

"Not *that* song." I picked up the handheld computer from where Sam had propped it on my desk. Damocles's image zipped around the room until I steadied it again. "Listen. The buses aren't running, so my mom's probably not coming home tonight. We can walk to the Stellar building, but it'll take a couple of hours."

"We?" Sam jumped down from the bed. "I'm going, too?"

"I can't leave you here alone." I looked at Damocles as he hovered a few inches above the floor. "Any advice before I shut you off?"

"First, take whatever you can carry from my belt, especially Mastix. I'll teach you how to revive it and use it."

I glanced at the whip where I had laid it on my desk, its thongs still dark.

"Second," he continued, "you'll have to be sneaky. Assume Mephisto saw the ad, so he'll be watching for me. Because of your age, you might be able to slip past his spies right under their noses. Just watch out for anything and everything. You're smart. Use your brains."

I nodded. "Easy to say. Hard to do."

"Nothing heroic is ever easy." He crossed his muscular arms over his chest. "Heroes often have to do hard things."

I looked at his serious expression. He was right. If I wanted to be a hero, I had to forget about the danger and just do it. "Okay. Thanks. Anything else?"

He shook his head. "You can turn me off now. Bring me back anytime you need me."

"All right. Thanks again." I turned the projector off. Damocles faded and disappeared.

Sam blinked at me. "That was as cool as fruit-punch ice cubes."

"Yeah. Tell me about it." I altered to an energetic tone. "Okay, let's grab a quick dinner and get going."

"Cold pizza's fast." Sam scurried out of the bedroom in a flash.

After putting my watch back on, I grabbed the two gadget belts — Damocles's and mine — and laid them on my bed. Several items on his belt were blackened or melted, but I found a small working flashlight and an auto-reel spool. That would come in handy because I had only one loaded spool left. Using their built-in clips, I fastened the gadgets and the computer combo to my own belt and wrapped it around my waist.

Bouncing on my toes, I tested the load. Too bulky. I detached the paintball gun and empty spool and retested the load. Not great, but it would work.

Just as I tightened the strap, the building began shaking again. I set my feet and shouted, "Sam! Another earthquake!"

CHAPTER 7

Sneaking Through the Dead Zone

I clipped Mastix to my belt and staggered to the kitchen. Sam stood motionless with a slice of pizza dangling from her mouth, her arms and legs spread. The ceiling cracked. Above her head, a big chunk of wallboard dropped. I grabbed her wrist and jerked her out of the way just before it crashed to the floor.

Still holding her wrist, I ran with her into the hall, down the stairs, and out the main entry. We stood under a portico where cars drop off passengers. Sirens wailed. Horns honked. People ran from place to place, some quiet, some shouting.

The ground shook even harder. The portico's support columns broke. The roof collapsed. I dropped to a crouch and tried to pull Sam down, but she stood firm. The pizza still in her mouth, she caught the roof in her uplifted hands and held it aloft. Although her brow bent, her arms didn't even tremble.

"Run," she said, mumbling through the pizza.

I scrambled on all fours. When I got out of the way, she threw the roof. The ten-foot-by-ten-foot slab of wood and concrete hit the pavement and broke into three pieces. Dust flew everywhere.

Her brow still bent, Sam walked toward me and pulled out the pizza. "Now it's dirty."

I rose and glanced around. As the tremors continued, people ran in every direction. It seemed that no one noticed Sam's superhuman feat. "Thanks," I said. "Sorry about the pizza."

"So I eat a little dirt." She brushed sand from the slice and took a big bite.

Barney ran out of our building and halted where the portico used to be. He stared at us wide eyed. "Eddie, Samantha, you made it!"

"Yeah. We're fine." Bracing my feet against the trembling ground, I scanned the rest of our building. It still seemed pretty solid for the most part. "How's everything inside?"

The moment I asked the question, people began streaming out the door with suitcases and armloads of belongings. "Not good at all," Barney said. "We're evacuating."

"Where will everyone go?"

"To the shelters. Stronger buildings." He withdrew a harmonica from his jeans pocket. "Think you can walk to Magruder's to be with your mom?"

"No problem. Sam and I have walked there lots of times."

"Good. You can get there before dark." Barney blew a high note on the harmonica. "Listen, everyone. I have a list of shelters."

While he talked, I imagined the cracks in our ceiling getting longer and wider. My superhero generator might not be safe, but what could I do? We had to get to the roof of the Stellar building … if it still stood.

"Let's go." I took Sam's hand, and we walked briskly on the sidewalk toward Magruder's, the tremors lessening along the way. When we came upon a truck that had careened off the road and slammed into a streetlamp, blocking our path, we shifted to the road. Since it was filled with cars that couldn't go anywhere because of the massive traffic jam, we weaved around them until we were well out of Barney's sight.

Sam swallowed the last bite of her pizza. "Can we get more food at Magruder's?"

"Most likely." Ahead, two men shouted nose to nose next to their smashed vehicles, looking like they were ready to punch each other. Still hand in hand, we ignored them, squeezed between a Jeep and a pickup truck, and hurried on.

We angled back to the sidewalk and stopped at an intersection where another sidewalk led to the right into a park where we sometimes went — Sam for the swings and me for the skateboard ramps — a good shortcut to get downtown. We also tent camped there twice every summer before Dad …

I buried the thought. This was no time to think about the past.

As I looked around, something felt strange. The tremors had stopped quite a while ago, but now the air was motionless. Car horns fell silent. Only a single siren wailed in the distance.

Sam tightened her grip on my hand. "What's happening, Eddie?"

"I don't know. It's weird." Far ahead, the city's skyline drew dark jagged lines across the horizon. A ball of blue light hovered over the tallest skyscraper — the Stellar building. The light expanded, adding colors as it morphed into the shape of a man's head. With dark beady eyes, hawkish nose, and sinister smile, it didn't take long to figure out who it was.

I whispered, "Mephisto."

In the midst of the stalled traffic, people got out of their cars and stared at the massive face. I turned on the handheld computer and lifted it to make sure the camera could view the scene. Damocles needed to see this.

The huge eyes shifted, as if surveying the silent city. The lips moved, and a voice boomed. "I am Mephisto, the mastermind who caused the recent earthquakes. I have a message for Damocles. Surrender to my demands by dawn, or Nirvana will meet its doom. Come to the Stellar roof at midnight with no weapons. This is my only warning."

The face collapsed back to a blue sphere and slowly faded away.

People standing near their cars gawked at the sky for a moment, then began talking to each other. Most of them seemed nervous or angry. Sam said something about Mephisto being ugly and scary, but I ignored her.

While the chatter continued, I stared at the Stellar building. Now Mephisto was calling for the meeting. What happened to Chet Graham?

Red-streaked clouds framed the fifty-story building. Soon the sun would set, and Sam and I would be walking in darkness. With so much panic and chaos, who could tell how dangerous it might be to go there?

I let out a sigh. It would be so easy to give up on this crazy adventure and just run to Mom for shelter. We could get hot food, sit in a corner booth and watch TV — let someone else take care of this menace. How could a couple of kids stop an insane villain like Mephisto? It was impossible.

Then Damocles's message came to mind. *Heroes often have to do hard things.*

His words stabbed deeply. I turned off the handheld computer, but that did nothing to ease the pain. Damocles trusted me to do this. How could I sit in comfort while Mephisto systematically destroyed Nirvana and maybe the entire world?

Sam tugged on my arm. "Eddie, you zoned out. Are we going to Magruder's or not?"

I shook my head. "We're not."

She laid a hand on her stomach. "But they have such good lasagna, and I'm still hungry."

"We'll find something else. I have money." I turned toward the park and marched straight ahead. "Let's go."

Sam jogged at my side. "What are we going to do about Mephisto?"

"We?" I laughed under my breath. "You'll hide somewhere while I use Mastix to stop him." I added in my mind, *if I can figure out how to use it.*

"But I'm the one with super powers, so I should be the one to do it." She slowed at a food cart that had toppled over. Hot dogs, relish, and plastic bottles of mustard and ketchup lay across the grass. Ants swarmed over the wieners and buns.

I hurried on. "Forget about it, Sam. I can't let you fight against the most powerful villain in the world."

"I can fight him better than Damocles's ghost can." She caught up and kept pace again, now with a hot dog in each hand. "So I eat a few ants."

Along the way, we hopped over huge cracks in the sidewalk, crossed streets that were either vacant or blockaded with immobilized cars, and dodged a couple of fallen trees. People ignored us, too busy chattering about the earthquakes and the image of Mephisto in the sky.

After stopping to get a drink from a spewing hydrant, we hurried on the main road leading to downtown, now abandoned. Soon, daylight faded to dusk, then dusk to darkness. The streetlamps stayed off. The only lights that remained were flashing blue police strobes ahead, enough to guide our way.

When we arrived, a tall police officer held up a hand. "Where are you two going?"

Sam spoke is a rasping voice. "To the Stellar building to stop Mephisto."

"Sam, give it a rest." I sighed and gave the officer a wink. "She thinks she's a superhero."

"Well, we need a superhero. No one's seen Damocles for quite a while." The officer picked up a Thermos from the top of his squad car. As he poured coffee into the lid, he looked at me with a sympathetic expression. "So why are you really out here? Lost? Can't find your folks?"

Sam spoke up again, her voice more raspy than

before. "I don't have any folks. I'm an orphan, and I need to see my cancer doctor."

"I liked the first lie better." He slurped his coffee. "Listen, kids, even if you do have to see a doctor, you can't get into the downtown district. It looks like Mephisto used his magna-gopher to uproot some of the roads and alleys. Electrical wires are exposed. Water lines are snapped. Just about every way to get there has some kind of hazard blocking it."

I arched my brow. "*Just about* every way?"

The officer waved an arm. "Well, from here all the way around to forty-fourth street, and in the other direction, from here to ninth. That leaves five safe blocks around the perimeter, but you'd have to go through the Dead Zone to get downtown." He smiled in the way most adults do when they're trying to scare kids to keep them safe. "Word has it that nine people have been murdered in that zone since the quakes started."

I gave him the kind of nod kids give to parents to calm their nerves. "You're right. It's dangerous. Too dangerous for kids like us."

Sam piped up, this time forgetting to disguise her voice. "It's not too dangerous for Princess Queenie Unicorn —"

I clapped a hand over her mouth. "We'll be going now, officer. Thank you."

"What's your name?" he asked. "I'll need to know when we find your mutilated bodies in the Dead Zone."

"Hertz."

"Yeah, it probably hurts to get mutilated, but if you'll tell me your name —"

"Our last name is Hertz. But don't worry. We'll leave." I took Sam's hand and walked away. Once we got deep enough into the darkness, we turned onto a path that would lead us to the Dead Zone.

"Where are we going?" Sam asked.

"To the Stellar building. We'll have to go through the Dead Zone to get there. But there's nothing to be afraid of. Like you were about to say, it's not too dangerous for ..." I glanced upward to recall the name. "For Princess Queenie Unicorn Esmeralda Sabrina Taryn Rosey Olive Buttercup Iris Tassels."

"No. You got it wrong again. My name is Princess Queenie Unicorn Olivia Tassels Emerald Rose Iris Pansies Sesame."

"Princess Quoterips?"

She growled. "If you don't stop that, I'm going to sing the Princess Queenie song the rest of the way to the Stellar building."

"All right. I'll stop. Anything to keep you quiet. If we make the slightest sound while sneaking through the Dead Zone, we might not come out alive."

"Don't worry, Eddie. I'll protect you." She flexed a bicep. "I've watched Princess Queenie fight lots of villains. I know what to do."

Now guided only by moonlight, we walked to a high chainlink fence and stopped. A broken gate stood open and partially blocked the way. In the darkness beyond, shadows flitted about — maybe branches moving in the breeze ... or bandits ready to pounce.

Sam shivered. "Maybe you should bring up Damocles so he can walk beside us."

"Not unless we need him. I don't want to run down the computer's battery before we get to the Stellar building."

"Okay … well … don't be scared, Eddie." Her grip on my hand tightened. "I'll make sure no one hurts you."

My ears warmed. Sam was scared, and I was a skinny wimp who had to count on his little sister to be the muscles in our duo.

I pulled Mastix from my belt and lifted it. The thongs stayed dark. Without the energy in the strands, I would be no more than a kid slapping the air with noodles.

I fastened it back in place. "Okay. We'll be fine. Just keep your head low."

We skulked into the Dead Zone and turned onto a walkway that led toward the Stellar building. As we traveled into a wooded area, tree branches obstructed the moon. Darkness shrouded everything. Even the walkway became almost invisible.

Sam spoke in a low tone. "I hear whispers."

"How many people? What are they saying?"

"Two, I think. One said something about kidnapping and ransom, and the other agreed. She also said a naughty word."

"She?"

"The first was a man. The second was a woman."

"Let's pick up the pace." Still holding her hand, I broke into a trot. Ahead, moonlight shone more brightly on the path. If we could just make it there, we would probably be all right.

Something tripped me. Just as I was about to topple headfirst, Sam pulled me back and held my arm.

A man stood in front of us. Moonlight peeked through the trees and shone on the blade of a long knife clutched in his hand. "Are you two lost?" he asked, his smile revealing gaps in his teeth.

"We're not lost." I tried to keep my voice steady. "Just passing through."

"Kids don't just pass through this place unless they're lost."

"Kirk, you're scaring them." A woman wearing heavy makeup stepped out of the shadows and joined the man. "These kids need a ride home. We can give them that, can't we?"

"Sure. No problem." Kirk slid the knife into a belt sheath. "I have a motorcycle with a side car. We can dodge all the traffic and get you home."

The woman extended a hand toward Sam. Long painted nails protruded at the ends of her wiggling fingers. "Come with me, sweetie, and we'll take —"

Sam grabbed the woman's wrist and jerked her to the ground. Before Kirk could react, Sam punched him in the stomach. He flew back, flipped through two reverse somersaults, and disappeared in the shadows.

I grabbed Sam's hand and shouted, "Run!"

CHAPTER 8

What Do You Say to a Super Villain?

We dashed toward the brighter part of the walkway, but several more shadowed figures stepped out of the woods and blocked our path.

"This way." I pulled Sam into the trees where we hunkered low in the darkness. "Keep your breathing quiet."

She spoke in halting gasps. "*Now* can you … make Damocles … walk next to us?"

Holding my breath, I unfastened the computer combo from my belt, turned the devices on, and brought up the image of Damocles, making sure his feet appeared to be touching the ground.

When the computer's camera activated, Damocles scanned the area. "Where are we?"

I inhaled quietly and whispered, "The Dead Zone. Near downtown."

Damocles's brow bent. "Why the Dead Zone?"

"It's the only way to the Stellar building where you were supposed to meet Chet Graham, and now Mephisto sent a holographic message in the sky demanding that you come there. Anyway, the earthquake blocked all the streets. We almost got kidnapped. And more muggers are waiting to jump us. So I dialed you up."

"You're a resourceful kid, Eddie." He pulled his cowl mask over his head and tucked in his dreadlocks. "Let's see what we can do to discourage the muggers."

I withdrew Mastix from my belt again. "I tried, but I couldn't get the thongs to light up. Did those bullets drain its power?"

"Only temporarily. It recharges itself from energy in the air." Damocles stared at the image of Mastix in his hand. "The power comes from your mind working with its programming. It hasn't made an attachment with you yet, because it doesn't recognize you as a superhero."

"A superhero? Can Sam use it?"

He shook his head. "While you held my wallet, your skin absorbed an encoded powder that made Mastix imprint with you, so it won't work with anyone else. As soon as it recognizes you as a superhero, it will revive."

"But how can I —"

"I'll explain more later. For now we'll have to count on my presence to scare the muggers." He nodded toward the walkway. "Let's go."

"C'mon, Sam." I held her hand and tiptoed out of the woods, keeping the projector steady at my side. Damocles moved his legs, as if striding with confidence, his phantom feet sweeping along the ground.

When we reached the moonlit path, whispers of *Damocles* shattered the silence. Running footsteps blended with the whispers, and fleeing shadows darted into the woods.

I shuddered. At least twenty villains scattered. We would never have made it, even with Sam's super strength. There were just too many of them.

"Keep your eyes focused ahead." Damocles said. "It's no shame to be scared, but there's no need to make them aware of your fear."

Sam clutched my hand more tightly. Her strength nearly crushed my fingers, but I stayed quiet.

When we reached the next border — another fence with a broken gate — we picked up the pace and exited to a wider sidewalk that ran parallel to a deserted road. With every streetlamp darkened, we again relied on moonlight to guide our way.

After a few minutes, we arrived at the front entrance of the Stellar building. I pointed at Damocles's holographic belt. "Mephisto said to come to the roof with no weapons."

"Good to know." He took off his belt and dropped it. When it hit the sidewalk, it vaporized. "Let's go in."

We climbed several concrete steps and stopped at a glass double door. I pulled the handle. Locked. "Sam, can you open it?"

"I'll try." She grasped the handle and pulled. The door's locking mechanism broke, and the door swung open. She smiled triumphantly. "Princess Queenie Unicorn Olivia Tassels Emerald Rose Iris Pansies Sesame does it again!"

I squinted at her. "You didn't change it this time."

"I never changed it. It's always been the same."

"Whatever." While Sam held the door, I walked into the building, still projecting Damocles at my side. Battery-powered emergency lamps in the ceiling corners lit our way to the stairwell. No use trying the elevators. They wouldn't be operating.

As we climbed the stairs, the corridor grew hotter, and the angle seemed steeper, though it had to be my imagination. When we finally reached the top, we came upon a ladder that led to a hatch in the ceiling. A corner lamp revealed an open padlock in the hatch's fastener. Good. No opportunity for Sam to show off again.

I climbed the ladder first. When I reached the top, I pushed the hatch and guided Damocles through the opening and onto the roof. When he had drifted several steps away, I set the projector down to keep him in place.

After Sam and I climbed out to the pebble-covered surface, I picked up the projector and skulked with her to an air-conditioning unit. We pressed our backs against the cool metal while I guided Damocles around the unit's corner. Moonlight shone on him as well as the light beam emanating from the lens, fading his image somewhat. Maybe Mephisto wouldn't notice it.

Sam poked my ribs and whispered, "I hear something. Sounds like a helicopter."

"Glad you have your super ears turned on. Let me know if you hear anything else unusual."

I looked at my watch — two minutes till midnight. Knowing that evil mastermind, he would be on time, and he would arrive in an unusual way — nothing as common as a helicopter.

Less than a minute later, a helicopter appeared and settled in a hovering position about a hundred feet over the roof. From its door, a searchlight beam swung across the roof until it landed on Damocles.

He raised a hand as if to block the light, though it couldn't really be blinding him.

Sam whispered, "Someone said, 'He's here. Proceed with the plan.'"

I glanced from the helicopter to Damocles and back again. No need to give him that update. He suspected some kind of sinister scheme.

Sam poked me again. "I hear wings flapping, like a huge bird."

"Even over the sound of that helicopter?"

She nodded.

I searched the sky. Since the Stellar building was the tallest in Nirvana and since nearly every light in the city was off, the moon provided a view of everything. So far, no bird appeared anywhere.

I looked at my watch again — twenty seconds till midnight. A shiver ran along my back. Soon, we would learn what Mephisto was planning.

With five seconds remaining, a glowing eagle flew into view to our left. The size of a small airplane, its wings thumped the air, sounding like a gorilla beating on a bongo drum. A man rode on its back, easy to see because of the eagle's luminescence.

It landed with a flurry and perched on the roof about fifty feet from us. The passenger climbed down and walked toward Damocles. Wearing feathery wings of his own, he stopped several paces away. Moonlight illuminated his hawk-like nose and evil grin. "Damocles," he said in a formal tone, "thank you for arriving on time."

I glanced at my gadgets belt. With Sam's strength and my spool lines, we could probably capture that fiend, but we needed to learn what this plan was all about.

Damocles crossed his arms. "I'm in no mood for your fake pleasantries. Just tell me what you want."

"To inform you that I am holding Chet Graham. Your delay in meeting with him proved to be costly. He was unable to hide from me any longer."

"All right. You informed me. Now what?"

"You have seen what I can do with Graham's technology, and you have the influence to collect the ransom money. Deliver one billion dollars in cash to this spot within three days or I will unleash an earthquake that will turn Nirvana into a heap of rubble. Then the ransom will jump to ten billion dollars, or I will destroy the entire world except for my secret fortress."

Damocles gave him a skeptical stare. "And how will you ensure that the technology is returned?"

"I have the only activation key for the mechanism's software. There is no way to save the programming code, duplicate it, or even read it. When you bring the money here, I will give you the mechanism at the same moment. Then I will no longer be able to employ the technology."

Damocles shook his head. "That's an old trick. I'm not stupid, Mephisto."

"Perhaps you would believe Graham." Mephisto waved a hand. A man wearing a suit and tie descended from the helicopter, dangling by a rope hooked to his belt. His hands and bare feet appeared to be bound as he swayed beneath the whipping propeller blades, his wiggling toes about ten feet from the roof.

The man shouted hoarsely, "Damocles, it's me! Chet Graham!"

The camera hummed and zoomed in on him while Damocles squinted.

A red icon flashed on the computer screen. Low battery. We had to get this meeting finished.

Damocles maintained a skeptical pose. "All right, Chet, what do you have to say?"

"He's telling the truth." The propeller chopped through Graham's words. "The software is safe. If we get the device back, he can't use the technology."

I pulled the razor-disk gun from my belt and aimed it at the rope. Since it shifted in the wind, hitting it would be tricky, but I had practiced with more difficult targets.

"Chet," Damocles said, "explain why you had an invention that destabilizes the earth. What good does that accomplish?"

"We were studying fault lines, running quake simulations in a tiny area so we could expand it on a computer to see who was most vulnerable. Our goal was to manufacture a warning device. The quake prototype was never intended to be used on a large scale."

"Yet it was able to —" Damocles's voice garbled.

Static filled his projected image. The battery was about to die.

I pulled the trigger. The razor disk shot out and nicked the rope a foot or so over Graham's head. Strands popped. The rope unraveled, but it didn't quite break.

Damocles disappeared.

Mephisto's gaze shifted until it landed on us. "Who are you?"

"We're busted." I reclipped everything to my belt and grabbed Sam's hand. "We'll run when I say go. Got it?"

She nodded, her stare locked on Graham.

Mephisto shouted toward the helicopter. "Damocles was a hologram. The real Damocles might be ready to attack." Then Mephisto and the eagle vanished.

I gasped. They were holograms, too!

"They're leaving," Sam said. "I have to save Mr. Graham." She ran across the roof and leaped toward him as he began rising higher with the helicopter. Her supercharged muscles sent her flying. She grabbed hold of his legs. The rope snapped, and they plunged together toward the roof.

CHAPTER 9

When Accidentally Going into the Girls' Restroom is a Good Thing

Graham landed on top of Sam. She let out a muffled squeal. When he rolled off, he curled on his side and groaned.

I ran to them. Sam lay spread eagle, a tight grimace on her face, though a smile broke through. She wheezed, "I did it."

"You almost got yourself killed!" My tone came out too harsh. She didn't deserve it. I heaved a sigh and extended my hand. "I'm sorry. C'mon Princess."

After I helped her rise, I withdrew a knife from my belt and cut the ropes binding Graham's wrists and ankles. He climbed to his feet, looked toward the sky, and growled. "The scoundrel escaped. I was hoping Damocles would catch him and put him away for good." He scanned the dim rooftop. "I saw the hologram. Where's the real Damocles?"

I brushed dark grit from Sam's shirt. "I'm not sure. I was surprised when he disappeared."

"That is his way." Graham stooped in front of Sam and smiled. "Thank you for rescuing me. Who knows what Mephisto might have done to me if not for you?"

She grinned. "You're welcome."

"Are you hurt?" He scanned her body. "Cuts? Bruises?"

"Just a headache, but I'm okay."

He looked her in the eye. "How in heaven's name were you able to jump so high?"

I barged in. "You weren't real high. It probably seemed higher because you were dangling from a chopper. And Sam's quite an athlete." I gave her a prodding look. "Aren't you, Sam?"

"Uh-huh." She winced. "But now I feel … kind of sick."

Graham touched the back of her head. "Might be a concussion. We'd better get her to a doctor." He scooped her into his arms and limped toward the roof's access door, wincing as the pebbly surface stabbed his bare feet. "I know a doctor who'll examine her."

"No!" I ran and caught up. "I need to get her to our mother. She'll take her to our family doctor."

"With traffic in a snarl and electricity out? That's not happening." He set Sam down on her feet next to the open trapdoor. "And besides, we need to contact Damocles so we can counter Mephisto's plot. Since you seem to be friends with him, I assume you can help me find him."

"Well … maybe."

"That's why we can't wait while you visit your mother. We're liable to have more earthquakes unless we stop Mephisto right away."

He talked to me like I was five years old. I hated

that. "It's not like I know his phone number or anything. He shows up when he wants to."

"I understand. But now he knows the circumstances. Maybe he'll find us."

After we made our way down the stairs and exited the building to the deserted street, Graham looked up at the dark sky. Moonlight illuminated his face, giving me a good look at his crew-cut hair and a short gash next to one eye that oozed a little blood. "Knowing Mephisto," he said, "he'll cause another earthquake soon, just to remind Damocles of his demands."

"Where is Mephisto's hideout? Since he captured you, you must know where it is."

Graham shook his head. "I was blindfolded until they lowered me from the helicopter."

"You couldn't even get a peek?"

"Not a chance. The blindfold was super tight."

I studied his profile again. The facial cut probably came from hitting the roof, but there was no sign of constriction from a tight blindfold. "So what do we do next?"

"Wait for Damocles to show up. He's the only one who can deliver the ransom and make sure Mephisto returns my technology."

"What? You expect Damocles to pay Mephisto?"

He gave me the old I'm-an-adult-so-I'm-smarter-than-you look. "Do you have a better idea?"

"Damocles will find Mephisto. Arrest him. Put him in jail."

"Good luck with that." Graham withdrew a phone from his pocket. "I need to make a call. Maybe the communication towers are operating by now." He walked several steps away and raised the phone to his ear.

I squinted at him. Why would Mephisto let a prisoner keep a phone?

"Sam," I hissed. "Listen in on his phone call and tell me what you hear."

"I'll try, but something's ringing in my ears." She trained her stare on Graham's back and relayed his end of the conversation. "Yeah, I'm all right. Just a cut. … No clue yet. But I'll find out what the kids know. … Don't worry. Damocles will get the cash. I'm sure he'll show up soon to check on the kids."

I whispered, "I don't like the sound of that." I slid my hand around Sam's wrist. "Let's get out of here."

When I pulled, she set her feet. "Why?"

"I think he's one of the crooks. Trust me. I'll try to explain later."

"All right. If you say so." We ran together back into the Stellar building and up the stairway, still lit by generator lights. As we climbed the steps, Sam gasped for breath. Her legs trembled. She wouldn't last much longer.

I lifted her and carried her fireman style. She didn't make a peep as she lay limply over my shoulders. I opened the door leading to the second-floor and stepped into a dark hallway.

With my hand against a wall, I searched for a door handle. When I came across one, I pulled the door open, walked in with her, and closed it behind us.

I put Sam down in a sitting position and settled next to her on a cool tile floor. Moonlight seeped through a window about ten steps away, illuminating her pain-streaked face. I brushed a tear from her cheek. "Are you injured?"

She squeaked, "I don't think so."

"Then what's wrong?"

"I dunno. I just feel sick."

"Maybe dirty pizza and ant-covered hot dogs."

"Maybe." Her voice altered to a whine. "I just want my mommy."

"We'll see her soon." I patted her knee. "Stay right here."

I rose and walked toward the window. Sinks lined one wall and toilet stalls the other. The absence of urinals told me more. We had stumbled into a girls' restroom.

When I reached the window's clear pane, I touched its frame — sealed. No way to open it. Outside, the wall led straight down to a street. All clear below.

From my gadgets belt, I unhooked the glass cutter — a diamond blade with a pen-like handle. Setting the blade against the pane and leaning into the effort, I cut a rectangular hole big enough for both of us. Just before finishing, I grabbed a suction cup from my belt, stuck it to the glass, and pulled on it while completing the cut.

Helped by a breeze from outside, I hoisted the carved-out section in and set it against a stall. Smoky air poured in, carrying the odor of an electrical fire.

With generators running city-wide, many accidental blazes were likely to sprout.

Sticking my head out the new opening, I looked below. A wide chasm ran straight down the middle of the street, and several cracks in the sidewalk made it look like someone had taken a jackhammer to it.

I mentally measured the vertical distance to the ground — about fifteen feet. We could do this. I walked back to Sam and helped her rise. "I need you to hang on to my back while I drop a spool line. Think you can do it?"

She nodded, her lips tight.

"Good girl." I stooped low. "Hop up."

She climbed onto my back and hung on. I hurried to the window, pulled a timed-release claw from my belt, and reeled out several feet of attached line. I attached the claw to a stall support and set the release timer for one minute. At that time, the claw's hooks would retract and let go of the anchor point.

As I retrieved gloves from my belt and put them on, I whispered to Sam, "You can do this. You're brave, just like Princess Queenie."

"I know," she said with a squeak, "but you're braver than me."

With my gloved hands clutching the newly cut edges of the opening, I stepped up to the window sill. Sam's weight made every movement harder.

I turned, swinging Sam out over the sidewalk. Holding the spool line with both hands, I rappelled down. Each time I pushed off the exterior wall, Sam grunted softly.

"Sorry," I whispered. "Can't slow down. Thirty

seconds till the hook releases. Don't want to slam butt-first on broken concrete."

Sam giggled. "You don't want to make your butt crack bigger?"

"Right. I don't want a gluteus cracksimus."

"What? I don't get it."

"Never mind. Now stay quiet. We're getting close." I glanced around. Moonlight revealed nothing but an empty city street in both directions. Graham was nowhere in sight.

The moment my feet touched down, the line went slack. Perfect timing. I pushed the button on the spool. The mechanism's whirring sound broke the silence as it slurped up the line. When the claw slapped against the spool, I pulled the laser pen from my belt and whispered, "Can you walk?"

"Maybe. For a little while."

I took her hand. "Let me know if you get tired. You can ride again."

While pointing the pen's narrow beam in front, I led Sam down the sidewalk. We dodged chunks of concrete as well as broken bricks, piles of shattered glass, and splintered boards that had fallen from various damaged buildings.

At one point, the debris blocked the walkway, piled too high to climb over. We detoured to the chasm in the middle of the street, found a narrow part, and jumped over it. At least Graham wouldn't be able to follow us. The rubble would slice his bare feet to pieces.

Soon, Sam grew tired again, and I let her ride on my back. I thought it best not to talk about her sudden loss of super strength, and since she didn't mention it, we just stayed quiet as we turned this way and that along quake-ravaged streets.

After a few minutes, we drew within two blocks of the police car we had seen earlier, though this time from the opposite side. As blue strobe lights swept past, I didn't bother trying to hide from the officer's view. Maybe we could get a ride somehow.

"I smell something," Sam said as we approached a corner. "Like a rotting dead dog."

"I don't smell anything." I stopped at the corner. After a few seconds, I smelled the odor. A flooded street blocked our way, and a bunch of rats swam in the water. The strong current kept some of them trapped in the flow while others scrambled to safety at each edge.

The police officer had mentioned the magnagopher uprooting the roads and breaking water lines, but the rats meant that the sewers had also ruptured, explaining the stink. The water was probably filled with filth, but the fast current indicated a shallow stream, though holes might be hiding almost anywhere under the surface.

Sam squeezed my shoulder. "Um … what do we do now?"

"I'm thinking." I searched the other side of the road for something that might hold a line claw, but all the streetlamps lay on the ground with their lamps submerged. Swinging over the flood wasn't possible. "We'll have to cross slowly. The rats will get out of the way."

"Okay …" Sam stretched out the word. "If you're sure."

"Right now I'm not sure about anything." I took

a tentative step. Cool water ran into my shoe and soaked my sock. From this spot, the water looked about ankle deep. "Help me watch for holes."

"Okay, but I hear something."

"What?"

"A man saying bad words. Like he's in pain."

I looked back. A human-shaped shadow appeared a block away, moving steadily toward us, though he stopped at times and rubbed a foot.

"Let's go." I walked straight into the flood, sliding my shoes and squinting at the flow to try to detect any holes. Rats swam out of my path. Dirty water rose to my calves, then to my knees. The current pushed against me, making it hard to lift a foot without losing my balance, especially with Sam wiggling on my back.

When I reached the halfway point, a man called from the rear. "Hey, you two! Stop!"

Graham's voice. I quickened my pace. Only five more steps and I could run on dry pavement. One step. Two. Three. When I set my foot down for number four, it plunged into deep water, and I face planted onto a swarm of rats and into the flood.

Sam's weight sent me under. With filthy water surrounding me, I couldn't breathe. Her arms tightened around my throat, pinching my blood supply. In seconds, I would pass out.

CHAPTER 10

What Do You Do When Your Save-the-World Device Needs Electricity but There's No Place to Plug it In?

Sam's grip loosened. Something latched on to my shirt and hoisted me up to shallow water. As I slid backwards toward the police car, I tried to turn my head to see who was dragging me, but I couldn't get the right angle. Who else could it be but Sam?

The car's spinning blue lights illuminated Graham as he trudged through the flood several paces away. I flipped over and jerked loose from my rescuer's grasp. Sam stood next to me in calf-deep water. She *did* rescue me.

"You must be feeling better," I said.

"I don't feel good at all." Her eyes rolled upward, and she collapsed with a splash.

I dropped to my knees and held her above the surface. Although she was breathing, her face looked ghostly pale in the blue glow. "Sam? What's wrong? Can you hear me?"

Her eyes stayed closed, and her breathing rasped, fast and shallow. I had to get her to Mom or maybe a hospital.

"Is she all right?" Graham called from the stream. "Did she faint?"

"Maybe." I rose to my feet, lifting her in my arms. Oily water streamed from her clothes and oozed across my skin. "I have to go."

"No. Wait. I'll help you." Graham set a foot forward. When it sank into the hole Sam and I had fallen into, he drew back. "Just stay put until I find a safe way across."

"Good luck with that." I walked alongside a relatively undamaged street toward the police car, guided by its flashing lights. If Graham really was in cahoots with Mephisto, maybe he would stay away from the police.

When we arrived at the car, I looked through its open driver's door, but no one was inside. Since the engine was running, the officer had to be close by.

I lifted Sam onto the driver's seat, then climbed onto the hood and looked around. Across the street, a uniformed man lay facedown on the sidewalk, his body sprawled over a fallen power line.

I jumped to the ground, ran to him, and dropped to my knees, not daring to touch him until I was sure he wasn't electrified. I jerked the laser pen from my belt and set the end against the back of his neck. The light stayed dark. No sign of electrical current in his body. I pressed a finger against his throat. His pulse thrummed, fast and jumpy. At least he was alive.

From the direction I had come, a shadow skulked closer. Could it be Graham? If so, I had to get back to the car and peel out as fast as possible, but I couldn't leave this officer here. He could die without help.

I rolled him to his back and patted his cheek. "Are you all right?"

"What?" He blinked rapidly. "I ... I can't see. Everything's black."

"Blindness from electrical shock. Let's hope it's temporary." I grabbed his arm. "I'll help you get to your car."

"Thanks." He sniffed. "Have you been wading in a sewer?"

"Something like that." After hoisting him to his feet, I held his arm as we walked. Every few seconds I glanced at the shadowy stalker. He now stood near a dark corner of a building, watching.

When we arrived at the car, I opened the rear door on the driver's side and helped the officer get in. Then I jumped into the driver's seat, pushed Sam to the passenger's side, and slammed the door. Gasping for breath, I looked at the officer. "Should I radio for help? An ambulance or something?"

"No use. Ambulances are trapped all across the city. The roads are a mess."

"I can drive. Just tell me where to go."

"Straight ahead. We cleared a road to a triage unit next to the Bingham hotel. Two doctors are there and four nurses."

"Bingham's the hotel with the statues of ducks, right? About three blocks from Magruder's."

"That's the place."

"Perfect. Our mom works at Magruder's. She's probably stuck there because of the quake. I have to find her."

"Hey, are you the kid with the sister who said she has cancer?"

"Yep." I shifted the stick to drive, and the doors locked automatically. "What about it?"

"You're too young to drive."

"So write me a ticket when we get there." As the car moved slowly forward, a hand slapped against my window. Another pulled on the latch.

Graham's face appeared on the other side of the glass, and his muffled shout filtered in. "You can't hide from me. I'll find out where Damocles is."

I extended a foot toward the gas pedal, but it wouldn't reach. I pushed a button that scooted the seat forward. With both hands on the steering wheel, I pressed the pedal down. The car lurched forward. Ahead, jagged cracks ran in crisscrossing patterns on the dimly lit street. Flares lay on the pavement at intervals of fifty feet or so. I slowed to a crawl to stay as close as possible to the guiding lights.

"I heard a man's voice," the officer said. "Who was he?"

I glanced at his inquisitive face in the rearview mirror. "Some guy who's been following my sister and me. He thinks we're friends with Damocles. I guess you heard that part. He's a nut case, I think."

"Nut case or not, we sure could use Damocles right about now. Someone has to stop Mephisto."

"Yeah. Someone has to." I touched my belt. If only I could power the computer up and check on Damocles. He could tell me what to do. But even if it had battery power, would it work after getting wet? Maybe. Maybe not.

Sam opened her eyes and whispered, "Where are we?"

"In a police car heading for the Bingham hotel. We'll be with Mom soon."

"Good." She grasped my arm with a cold, clammy hand. "I feel like a toothpaste tube someone stepped on. Like my stomach exploded and all my guts squirted out."

"That's … descriptive."

"But I didn't break the Princess Power Pledge. Honest."

"I know." I focused straight ahead at the line of flares. "Hang on. We should get there soon."

After a few minutes, I stopped where the flares ended in front of a huge statue of a decapitated duck with a police motorcycle parked next to it. Beyond this point, the pavement buckled everywhere, water spewed from deep cracks, cars lay on top of each other in a jumbled mess.

From a lamp atop a pole, a bright light streamed through the driver's side window, and noise from a generator drilled into my ears. "We're here," I called, loud enough to overcome the noise.

I shut off the engine and took the key, then opened my door and jumped out. About twenty paces away, even bigger light standards surrounded a massive tent. Under the canopy, dozens of people scurried around cots filled with moaning bodies. Other victims stood or sat with bandages wrapped around their heads or limbs.

An empty wheelchair stood near the closest tent. I dashed to it and rolled it back to the car. After I helped the officer get out, he grasped the chair's handles and braced himself. "My eyesight is starting to come back. I can wheel your sister to triage while you go and find your mother."

I glanced toward the path I had driven. "Will you stay with her? That stalker might show up."

"I'll stay. She'll be safe with me."

I helped Sam get out of the car, guided her into the wheelchair, then took off toward Magruder's. Once I had passed the triage area's perimeter lamps, the moon provided enough light to find my way down the street. Broken pavement, exposed pipes and wires, and a few shallow streams forced me to create my own meandering path. Fortunately, the electricity was off in this area, so I didn't have to worry about getting electrocuted.

When I reached Magruder's, I stopped at the front and looked through its big picture window. Light from a hundred candles flickered inside. Customers sat in every seat at every table, and two waitresses hustled back and forth. At least fifty people stood in the waiting area and formed a line that led out the open door.

I spotted a server who looked like Mom, though in the dimness I couldn't be sure. I headed straight into the waiting area and began muttering "Excuse me" as I squeezed between bodies. Just when I broke free and passed the cash register and its attendant, someone grabbed my arm.

"What's the hurry, Eddie?" I jerked loose and turned. Milligan stood next to the register. Still wearing a fedora and a gangster suit, he peeled a few bills from a roll and laid them in the attendant's hand. "Looks like you went for a swim." He inhaled through his nose. "In a sewer?"

"You're not the first person to ask me that."

"Where have you been?"

I growled, "None of your business."

"But it *is* my business, Eddie. I came by to get some food and had a nice chat with your mom. I told her I checked your apartment, and I couldn't find you. The quake broke your door, so I had a look around, but no Hertz kids."

I again spotted the server who looked like Mom, but she was someone else. "Where is she now?"

"She went home to find you. Just a couple of minutes ago. I told her I'd come and help as soon as I finished my midnight snack." He snatched a toothpick from a dispenser, poked it between his teeth, and stepped out of the way for the next person in line. "If you run, you might be able to catch her. I'd give you a ride, but my car's upside down on the corner of Kennedy and Fifth. A friend borrowed my motorcycle, so I had to walk here. Your building was on the way, so being a friend of your father's, I decided to check on you."

I looked at the register attendant and read her nametag — Judy. I had seen her a few times before. "Judy, is my mom still here?"

She shook her head as she collected a payment. "Like this guy said, she left a few minutes ago to look for you."

"All right. Thanks." I spun and headed straight for the door.

"Hey, Eddie," Milligan called, "Let me walk with you. The streets are getting dangerous."

"I'll take my chances." This time the crowd parted for me, remembering my odor.

When I got outside, I bolted to the triage area. I ducked under the tent and found Sam sitting in the wheelchair, slurping purple Gatorade through a straw from a plastic bottle. The officer lay on an elevated cot while a tall black woman wearing green scrubs bent over him, looking at his wounded eyes through a scope.

I snatched the Gatorade bottle from Sam and whispered, "You're allergic to the dye."

"That doctor said I'm dehydrated." Sam pointed at the woman in scrubs. "So give it back."

She reached to grab it, but I swung it away. "We'll find some water."

"Is there a problem here?" The doctor stood facing me, hands on her hips. Her sour expression said she didn't want to put up with any nonsense.

"No, ma'am." I gave the bottle back to Sam. "I'm here to take my sister home."

"Not a chance. She needs to stabilize. Her blood pressure is low. No sign of internal bleeding, but I still need to check her for infection."

A bright light flashed through the tent's canopy, and a voice boomed from the sky. "Damocles, I know you can hear me, so listen carefully."

When the doctor turned her head, I wheeled Sam from underneath the tent and looked toward the light. Mephisto's holographic face hovered over the city skyline. "The people of Nirvana think you're a hero, but you sent two children instead of negotiating with me yourself." The image let out a tsking sound. "How pathetic. The great Damocles has lowered himself to hiding behind a boy and a girl."

I clenched a fist but stayed quiet. It wouldn't do any good to shout a protest to a hologram.

"Damocles," Mephisto continued, "I know who those children are and where they live, so they cannot hide from me for long. If you value their lives, return to the Stellar roof to deliver my price. Otherwise, they will die, and Nirvana will experience an earthquake that will make the last one feel like the beating of a hummingbird's wings.

"As a warning, I will give the city another taste of my power. Set your watches. The warning shake will begin in two hours. If you don't show up within one hour after that, I will hit the city with the big one."

The hologram shrank and vanished.

I looked at my watch — 1:04 a.m. The warning shake would come at about 3.

"Damocles is a coward," a woman said.

A man spat on the road. "I always said he's nothing but a clown wearing a cowl."

A second man shoved the first man's arm. "You don't know what you're talking about. Damocles saved my daughter from a mugger. He's always been good for Nirvana."

While several more joined in the argument, I grabbed Sam's hand. "Stay quiet. We're going home." With the Gatorade bottle in hand, she rose from the wheelchair and skulked with me out of the light. As we drew close to Magruder's, I searched the area for Milligan. Maybe he decided to try to follow me home. If so, I didn't want to run into him.

I guided Sam toward a side street that led to an alternate route. It was a bit longer, but at least we would be alone. As expected, we ran into plenty of obstacles — downed streetlamps, water-covered roads, and huge cracks in the pavement.

Soon, three shadowy figures standing under a torn awning began following us. I touched my razor-disk gun. If I were alone, I could fight these guys, but I couldn't risk letting Sam get hurt.

I halted and stooped low. "You'd better ride."

Still clutching the half-empty Gatorade bottle, Sam climbed onto my back and wrapped her arms around my neck. The bottle's plastic rubbed against my cheek, but if I told her to throw it away, that might start an argument.

I straightened, grabbed her ankles, and took off in a trot, glancing back. The shadowy figures accelerated. One carried a baseball bat.

I searched for a place to disappear — a fire escape, an open window, any cover of darkness. But every possible spot was easy to see from the road.

Focusing straight ahead, I pushed my legs harder. On my back, Sam trembled, but she stayed quiet. Her weight dragged me down. I couldn't run much farther.

Just two blocks away, moonlight shone on the back side of our alley. Pounding footsteps from the rear fueled my jets. I rushed forward, turned the corner into the alley, and stopped under our fire escape.

As I reeled line from a spool on my belt, I looked

back. Shouts and grunts erupted from around the corner, but I had no time to investigate. I slung the line's clawed end up to our landing and waited while it twisted around the railing.

"Nice throw, Eddie."

The call came from a dark corner. By now, I recognized that voice. Milligan. "Were you one of those guys following us?" I asked.

"No." Milligan walked out of the darkness, a baseball bat in hand. "But I did make sure they stopped following you. One cracked skull, and the vermin scurried away."

"Why did you help?" I grasped the spool line and gave it a tug. It was secure. "What do you care?"

"I'm sort of the neighborhood watchman. I take care of my friends ... and their kids." He nodded toward the building. "Are you sure it's stable? It might collapse at any minute."

I scanned the structure. It seemed sturdy enough. Two kids weren't going to make much of a difference. "Thanks for the warning." I pushed a button on the spool. As I hung on, the mechanism reeled in the line and drew Sam and me up to the landing. I grabbed the rail and whispered to Sam, "Can you get to the platform?"

"I think so." While I guided her, she climbed onto the landing, then I swung up and joined her. As I unhooked the anchor, I looked down at Milligan.

He stared back at me. "Now what? I don't think your mom's there anymore."

"Maybe not, but I have to check."

"Whatever." Milligan shrugged. "If the building

collapses on you, I'll help dig your dirty, bloody corpses out for your grieving mother. And I'll tell her I warned you."

"You do that." I tried to open the bedroom window. Locked. Barney must have fixed it, but that wouldn't stop me.

I used the glass cutter to slice through the pane, reached in, and turned the lock. After helping Sam climb inside, I joined her in the dark bedroom and used my penlight to look around. Deep cracks ran along the ceiling and every wall. Another quake might make it crumble like a hammered cracker. I had to get the superhero invention out of my closet before that could happen.

I detached Damocles's miniature flashlight and extended it to Sam. "Look for Mom, but watch your step. The floor might have fragile spots."

As she took the flashlight, her hands trembled. The Gatorade in her bottle quivered with the motion.

"Hey." I compressed her shoulder. "You're Princess Queenie Unicorn ... Olivia ... whatever. You can do this."

She whispered a weak, "I know."

"Go on, then."

She turned and walked toward our bedroom door. "Mom?" she called. "Are you here?"

Guided by my penlight, I slid my desk chair into the closet and climbed onto the seat. I pushed open the low drop-ceiling panel and loosened the wing-nuts that fastened my invention to the ceiling's frame.

After unplugging the power cord, I grabbed

the unit's handle and hauled it down, careful to avoid scratching its ray-emitting lens. The size and shape of a portable search lamp, the entire module weighed only about five pounds. No problem.

The penlight's thin beam landed on the *A* logo on the unit's side, an adhesive decal I had applied to identify it if needed. I climbed off the chair and shifted the light toward the window. Lifting the unit through that opening wouldn't be hard, but it would be even easier to take it through the lobby. Maybe Mom was looking for us there. Or Barney might be around, and he could tell me if he had seen her.

Carrying the superhero unit with one hand and pointing the pen's light in front, I walked out of the bedroom and toward the outer hall. As Milligan had said earlier, our door was broken, barely hanging by a hinge.

Sam's light beam flashed from the kitchen. "I can't find Mom anywhere."

"Let's look downstairs. Follow me." With Sam close at my heels, I walked to the stairwell and down to the lobby. Beyond the exit doors, Barney paced outside, a rifle propped against his shoulder as if he were a military sentinel.

Not wanting Barney to see the superhero unit, I set it down behind the lobby's front desk, took Sam's hand, and hustled outside with her. "Barney, have you seen my mother?"

He halted with a gasp. "Where have you been? Your mother was here looking for you. I took her up to your apartment, but we couldn't find you."

"I just got here." I glanced around, but darkness

veiled everything except the debris from the collapsed portico. "Where did she go?"

"Back to Magruder's. At least she headed that way. I told her I'd watch for you."

I squinted at the rifle. "Heavily armed, I see."

"The building's been evacuated. No power. No water. I'm standing guard against looters."

"No power. That's not cool." I glanced back at my invention. Somehow I had to get access to electricity. "Do you have a generator?"

Barney nodded toward the lobby. "Next to the front desk. Not much gas left. I'm saving it in case of an emergency."

"Can it handle a ten-amp draw?"

"I think so. Why?"

"I have an emergency. So, if you don't mind."

"What kind of emergency?"

I took a deep breath. "I have to save the world."

CHAPTER 11

What Happens When You Plug in a Superhero?

Two flashlights, Damocles's and Barney's, lay on the lobby floor and illuminated Barney's generator as it chugged and coughed. Smoke poured from its exhaust pipe and up to the high ceiling where it seeped through big cracks and filtered out.

I plugged the superhero invention's lamp module into one of the generator's outlets and my computer power adapter into another. Getting Damocles back into commission was probably the most important thing I could do. The world needed him.

I set the computer on the floor. While it charged, I positioned the lamp so that the lens pointed at me. I could try it on myself, but since it didn't work before, it was better to let Sam be the superhero again. As weak as she was, she needed the boost.

"So what's this gizmo?" Barney asked, pointing at my invention.

"Well ..." I took Sam's hand and pulled her in front of the lens. Somehow I had to create a diversion. "Hey. Do you have anything to eat? Sam's going to be really hungry."

"*Going* to be hungry? How do you know?"

"Just trust me. If you don't want her to eat your shoes, you'd better find something."

"Okay. Whatever." Barney shrugged. "I have a peabudill in a cooler in my truck. She can have that."

"A peabudill?"

"It's short for a peanut butter, mayonnaise, and dill pickle sandwich. Tastes great, but the texture is like chewing cockroaches. You kind of have to get used to it."

I resisted the urge to cringe, and I definitely didn't want to ask how he knew what chewing cockroaches felt like. "That'll do."

When he exited the building, I set my hands on Sam's shoulders and looked her in the eye. "Are you ready? I mean, you don't have to do this."

"I'm ready." Her weak voice barely rose above the generator's racket. "I want to be Princess Queenie again. I have to stop Mephisto."

"All right, then." I released her and stooped beside the superhero device. With a finger on its power switch, I gave her a nod. "Close your eyes."

When she complied, I flipped the switch. Bright light flashed from the lens and bathed Sam in an ultra-white glow. Her entire body looked like the negative of a photograph, and her bones appeared through her skin and clothes.

The generator whined. Obviously, the amperage draw was putting a strain on it. It might not last much longer. After a few more seconds, my invention's auto-timer shut the light off, and the unit powered down. The generator sputtered and coughed, then died. Silence descended in the lobby.

I rose and took Sam's hand. "You can open your eyes now."

She looked at me and smiled. "I feel a lot better."

"Do you have your strength back?"

She lifted an arm and flexed her bicep. The muscle swelled and bulged. "Yep. I'm Princess Queenie Unicorn Ariel Kitten Emerald Sesame Lilac Iris Pony again."

"Princess Quakeslip? That's a new one."

"No, it's not." She uncapped the Gatorade bottle. "I'm starving."

"Yeah, I thought that might happen. Barney will be back with something in a minute." I unplugged the handheld computer from the generator and looked at the battery meter — about 20% charged. "Let's see what Damocles has to say."

"Look who I found." Barney walked in with Mom at his side.

"Eddie! Sam!" Mom ran to us and pulled us both into a hug. "Where have you been? I was so worried about you."

"We came here looking for you," I said.

Mom drew back and wrinkled her nose. "It smells like you've been wrestling with pigs."

"We kind of took a spill in a —"

"And Sam's arms. She's swollen again." Mom took the Gatorade bottle from her. "Purple Gatorade? You know she's —"

"I know, Mom. I know." I wrestled free from her grasp. I had to figure out how to escape so we could get to the Stellar building. "Mom, don't they still need you at Magruder's? I heard it's like an emergency shelter now."

"They do. Supposedly we're going to have another earthquake in ..." She looked at her wristwatch. "Just under one hour. So I need to get you there. If any building can stand another quake, Magruder's can."

I mentally pictured the restaurant and the nearby triage area. If the police car was still there, Sam and I could go for another ride on the cleared road and walk the rest of the way. "That's perfect, Mom, but how do we get there before the quake hits? No car can get around all the damage on the roads."

"No, but bicycles can."

"Bicycles? We don't have —"

"Yes, we do. I bought three bikes with some of the money you gave me. You've been asking for one for months." She pointed toward the door with her thumb. "Barney has them in his truck."

"Sure do." Barney pulled a wrapped sandwich from his pocket and extended it toward Sam. "And here's the peabudill I promised you. Your mom said it shouldn't make you react."

Sam took the sandwich and began tearing the wrapping off. "Thanks."

Mom pointed at my belt. "What are those gadgets you're wearing?"

"Superhero gear. You know, to stop Mephisto from destroying Nirvana."

"I love your imagination." She patted me on the head in the most annoying way possible. "Keep aspiring to great things, Eddie."

I ducked out of her reach. "Sure, Mom. I'll do my best."

"We'd better hurry." Mom took Sam's hand. "Time's running short."

I snatched Damocles's flashlight and the computer from the floor and attached them to my belt. But I had to leave the superhero generator behind — too awkward to carry while riding a bike. "Mom, why don't you and Sam and Barney get the bikes? I'll meet you in the parking lot in a minute."

"Why? What do you have to do?"

I altered to an excited-little-kid's tone. "I have to hide my superhero generator so Mephisto won't find it."

"Okay, Eddie. Whatever you say." Mom, Sam, and Barney walked outside.

As soon as they were out of sight, I picked the unit up by its handle and set it behind the lobby's front desk. When I emerged, Milligan walked in.

He smirked. "Whatcha doin' back there, Eddie? Hiding?"

I concealed a swallow. I couldn't let him know the truth. He might steal my invention. "Yeah. Hiding."

"Not so brave without your superhero disguise, huh?"

I altered to a timid voice. "Yeah, it's pretty scary out there. The ground's been shaking a lot."

"Don't try to con me, kid. I saw you swing across the skyline like Tarzan. You're not scared of a few jiggles in the ground."

"Well, they felt pretty strong to me." I marched toward the door. "I gotta go."

"Suit yourself, but I'm keeping my eye on you. I have to be a watchdog for a poor family that doesn't have a dad around, you know."

I exited and walked toward the parking lot, looking back to see what Milligan would do. He sauntered out and headed in the opposite direction. Good. My invention was safe.

After Barney unloaded three bicycles from his pickup truck — blue for me, red for Mom, and pink for Sam — he opened the truck's passenger door and produced three backpacks with the same colors.

Sam clapped her hands. "New backpacks!"

"And color coordinated," Mom said.

After Mom and Sam put on their backpacks, Barney handed me the blue one. "You might want to stick your gadgets in there. Tough riding with stuff dangling near the spokes."

"True." I took the backpack and transferred most of the gadgets from the belt to the pack's main pouch, including the flashlight, the computer/projector unit, and Mastix, though I left the two spools attached. They wouldn't dangle, and having them handy might be a good idea.

All that stuff made the backpack pretty full, but I might be able to fit the superhero device in there. I just needed an excuse to go back and get it.

"Let's hurry," Mom said as she climbed on her bike and pedaled away. "They need me at Magruder's right away." Sam jumped onto her bike and followed.

Sighing, I followed as well. Without a decent excuse, I just had to hope the device was safe behind the desk. No one who found it would think it's valuable anyway.

Along the route, we dodged holes, ditches, and wrecked cars. Once we had to ride through water that rose halfway up our wheels, but we managed. Sam kept surging in front, her powerful legs giving her a boost, but with a few scolding looks, I finally convinced her to stay at a normal kid's speed.

As we wheeled along, a feeling that we were being watched made my skin crawl. I looked back every few seconds. Maybe Milligan was following us again. But how? No car could navigate all of these obstacles.

When we arrived at the restaurant, we squeezed our bikes through the crowd in the lobby and parked them inside next to the front window. After we used the restrooms, Mom set us at a two-person booth and gave us each a meatball sub.

Sam downed hers in about a minute and a half. While I munched on mine and watched Mom bustle back and forth among the customers, I estimated the time it would take to bike to the Stellar building — probably fifteen minutes.

I glanced at the clock on the wall, a circular analog face with beer bottles for hands — 2:40 a.m. My wrist watch said the same. Twenty minutes till the next quake. Since I still had to talk to Damocles, we couldn't afford to lose another second.

The moment Mom disappeared into the kitchen, I stuffed the last bite of my sandwich into my mouth and whispered to Sam in a bread-garbled voice, "It's time to go."

Our heads low, we skulked to the waiting area,

grabbed our bikes, and walked them outside. Once on the street, we hopped onto the seats and took off toward downtown.

After we passed the triage area, we came upon the police car and a motorcycle parked next to the decapitated duck. Chet Graham sat in the car's driver seat with the officer on the passenger's side. When Graham saw us pass by, he jumped from the car, leaped onto the motorcycle, and kick started it.

I pulled a few feet of line from a spool and reached the claw toward Sam. "Attach this and take off like a rocket."

Grinning, she grabbed the claw and hooked it to her bike's frame. She then leaned forward and churned her legs like a pair of hot-rod pistons. After giving her a short lead, I locked the line, lifted my feet from the pedals, and hung on.

When the line tightened, my bike and I surged ahead. Angling this way and that, Sam dodged holes, fallen streetlamps, and trapped cars.

I looked back. As the motorcycle dodged the obstacles, its headlight weaved from side to side. The light's glare made it impossible to see Graham's face, but I imagined a threatening scowl.

The headlight drew closer and closer. Sam was fast, but she was dragging too much weight. I called out, "I'm cutting myself loose. Go to the Stellar building. I'll meet you there."

I detached the line and let it fly. Sam shot ahead while I drifted back until I stopped. Just before Graham's motorcycle caught up, I turned my bike ninety degrees and leaped out of the way. The bike slid under his front tire, and the motorcycle slung him forward over the handlebars. While he flew, the two bikes tangled and flipped again and again before skidding to a stop.

Darkness shrouded the street ahead. No sign of Sam or Graham. I ran in the direction we were going. As I passed my bicycle, I looked it over. It had twisted into a blue metallic pretzel. So much for my gift from Mom.

About thirty feet farther down the road, I found Graham sprawled across broken pavement, his face bloodied. I check his throat pulse. He was alive, but he seemed to be unconscious.

I jogged on, dodging puddles and leaping over jutting concrete as I called out, "Sam? Where are you? Can you hear me?"

When I reached the ditch where I had fallen earlier, I halted and looked beyond it. Sam was a stubborn squirt. If she decided to go to the Stellar building like I told her, nothing would stop her.

I glanced at Graham, now fifty feet back. He lay motionless. I couldn't just leave him there, could I? He might be bleeding internally. He could die.

But this guy was a first-class creep, the bad guy, the villain. Probably almost as evil as Mephisto. I could leave him without another twinge of guilt.

I searched the area for something to build a bridge with. After finding a few broken two-by-fours and setting them over the ditch, I tiptoed across and ran toward the Stellar building, alternately looking at its roof and the ground, both illuminated by moonlight.

When I drew within a couple of blocks of the

building, the pavement ahead buckled. The ground shook and lurched from side to side. I dropped to my knees and grabbed a fallen light pole. The Stellar building cracked down the middle. Half of it fell to the side and crumbled over a lower building's roof, sending a rolling river of dust toward me.

I crouched and turned my back to it. The river blasted into my body, coating me with dirt. When the dust settled, I turned toward the building again, coughing as I shouted again, "Sam? Where are you?"

I staggered toward the Stellar's remains, the quake pitching the ground and making me feel like a seasick sailor on a storm-tossed ship deck.

Then, the quake stopped.

Dizzy, I tried to walk straight ahead, but the road still seemed to waver. I stopped at every intersection and looked both ways, calling for Sam, but no one answered.

After several stops and futile calls, I came upon a fire hydrant that spewed water into a huge gorge. Since it was at least twenty feet wide, I couldn't jump over it, and the gorge's ends were out of sight, making it impossible to go around it.

I stepped close and looked down. The gushing water spilled into the depths, too dark to see anything more than a few feet below.

Something glimmered to my right. Several steps away, a pink bicycle lay near the edge with the spool line lying on the street.

My throat cramped. Sam?

CHAPTER 12

Sometimes a Sister is Pretty Cool to Have Around

I shouted into the gorge. "Sam? Are you down there? Can you hear me?"

The roar of gushing water drowned my voice.

I grabbed the spool line's claw from the bike frame and attached it to the fire hydrant. After getting my gloves from the backpack and putting them on, I clutched the line with both hands and rappelled down the side of the gorge.

As I slid lower and lower into darkness, I called out for Sam again and again, but the deafening sound of crashing water overwhelmed my shouts.

Since I had detached the line from the spool while we were riding our bikes, I wouldn't be able to auto-reel the line when the time came to climb back out of the gorge. Of course, I could manually rewind the line into the spool and reset the spring, but that required special tools I had at home. I should've used my other claw and spool. Too late for that now.

When I touched down, I stood in a cold, knee-deep rush of water. I pulled the flashlight from the backpack, flicked it on, and cast the beam around. No sign of Sam.

Downstream, the river hurtled into darkness.

Upstream, the waterfall from the hydrant above splashed onto bare rock, birthing the shallow river and a wall of misty spray. Behind the cascading curtain, the ground appeared to be dry. Sam was smart enough to go that way.

I sloshed upstream and dodged the cascade, though the spray dampened my hair and face with tiny droplets. As I walked on, I swept the beam from side to side, checking for any sign of a girl with super strength, but only dark rock appeared in every direction.

When the splashing noise lessened, I ventured another call. "Sam? It's Eddie. Can you hear me?"

My voice echoed off the walls, but no answer from Sam. I pivoted and looked back at the tumbling water. How far should I go? Maybe she didn't fall in. Maybe she ditched the bike and jumped over the gorge. If she made it to the Stellar building, she might have been crushed when it collapsed.

I heaved a sigh. Just one hundred steps more. If I didn't find Sam, I would turn back and try to climb out.

Counting my paces, I walked on. Above, the opening vanished. I was now in a tunnel that turned in the direction Sam and I had been biking. When I reached eighty steps, a light appeared far ahead. It looked like the end of the tunnel — a circular opening into some kind of underground chamber.

I stopped. Based on my memory of the city map, that chamber was right under the Stellar building, or what was left of it. Keeping my footfalls quiet, I hurried on.

As I drew nearer, the sound of a motor grew louder and louder. I ran to the opening, hid behind the wall, and peered around it. The chamber, little more than a cavity carved out of the rock, appeared to be about twenty feet in both length and width and eight feet high.

The light came from a table lamp lying on the floor, probably toppled by the quake. Its power cord led to a generator sitting near a wall on the left side. As it chugged, its exhaust funneled into a pipe protruding from the wall. To the right, Sam lay curled on a gray upholstered sofa, her eyes closed and her head on her backpack.

As I hurried toward the sofa, I came upon a big hole in the floor and ran around it. I could check it out later. I knelt at Sam's side and patted her hand. "Sam? Are you all right?"

Her eyes fluttered open. She winced and spoke with a squeak. "No. I feel sick again. Worse than ever, like I'm going to puke."

I attached the flashlight to my belt. "Is your super strength gone already?"

"Mostly. I heard you calling me, though. And I answered. Didn't you hear me?"

"No. It was too noisy." I laid a palm on her forehead — feverish. Compressing lightly, I felt her arms and legs for signs of broken bones. When I touched her right ankle, she groaned.

I pulled up her pant leg. A bruise colored her ankle purple and black. As I wiggled her foot, her grimace tightened. "It might be broken," I said. "Or maybe badly sprained."

She inhaled dramatically. "Princess Queenie Unicorn Iris Ponyrider Buttercup Olive Lover Rosey Is Posey has been injured. What will she do now?"

"Why did you go back to the original name?"

"Go back? It's been the same all the time."

"No, it hasn't. You changed it to —" I shook my head. "Never mind."

"My other ankle hurts, too."

As I pulled up her left pant leg, I said, "So what will the princess do now that she's injured?"

"Princess Queenie is a humble lady. She would ask Damocles for help."

"You're right. Let's ask him." After examining her other ankle, also bruised, though not as badly, I pulled my backpack off, withdrew the computer-projector unit, and turned it on.

When it powered up, Damocles appeared. He stood next to me, his cowl mask in place as he looked around. "Where are we, Eddie?"

"Under the Stellar building, I think." I gave him a quick rundown of recent events. Sam added her side of the story, including her fall into the gorge. Since she landed flatfooted, even her super strength couldn't keep her ankles from getting hurt.

"I heard a motor running and followed it to this room," Sam said. "I felt sicker every minute, so when I saw this sofa, I knew exactly what to do. Collapse."

Damocles looked up at the rocky ceiling. Deep, jagged cracks zigzagged from corner to corner. "This chamber is too primitive and fragile to be Mephisto's hideout."

I kicked a stray pebble and watched it roll into the hole I had seen earlier. "Since this place is underground, could it be a parking spot for his magna-gopher? It could be a central location to send it out to carve up the city."

Damocles pointed at the hole. "Then what might that be?"

I walked to the edge and looked into the depths. Shining the light into it revealed nothing but darkness. "It's pretty big. Maybe the gopher left that way. Part of a network of tunnels."

"An excellent thought. Mephisto is preparing for the biggest shake yet by undermining the foundations, making it easier for buildings to collapse."

I looked again at Damocles. "But how will you meet him now? The Stellar building's just a shell."

"He'll have to send another message, and he won't wait long. If he uses a sky hologram to give us instructions, he won't know that we can't see it."

"Then we have to get out. And fast. Sam's too weak to climb, and there's no way I can carry her up my line."

"Can't you auto-reel the spool?" Damocles asked.

I shook my head. "I detached, and I can't reload the spring without tools. I have another spool, but throwing a claw that far up is impossible."

"And if you stay here when the quake comes, you'll get crushed." Damocles looked Sam over. After a couple of moments, he gestured for me to come close and whispered, "Based on your explanation, it looks like her superpower charge didn't last as long the second time, and her sickness increased. If you give her a third dose, it would probably heal her and give her enough strength to get both of you out of here, but her power would be even shorter lived. I'm afraid she would get sicker than ever or perhaps die. The effect of the ionization on the body is unpredictable."

I nodded. "Either way, I don't have the superpower generator, so no use worrying about that."

Sam piped up. "I hear someone coming through the tunnel."

I spun toward the passage. A shadow appeared in the depths, growing larger as it approached.

"Do you have Mastix?" Damocles asked.

"Right here." I pulled it from the backpack and held it tightly as if ready to strike, but the thongs stayed dark.

Damocles furrowed his brow. "It still doesn't recognize you as a superhero. We'll need to find another option."

I returned Mastix to the pack. "Like what?"

"Turn me off for now. If this person causes trouble, then turn me back on. That should scare him away."

I switched off the projector and aimed its lens at the tunnel. Seconds later, Milligan walked in carrying my superhero generator by its top handle.

I gulped. "Milligan?"

He skirted the hole, stopped a few steps out of reach, and set the unit down. Now wearing jeans and a baseball jersey and cap instead of his gangster suit, he looked almost normal. With a fist on one hip, he took on a parent's scolding posture and tone. "Eddie, what are you doing down here?"

I squared my shoulders. "I was going to ask you the same question."

"I was just making sure you're safe. Climbing down that line wasn't easy, but I promised your mom I'd find you."

"Where is she now?"

He pointed over his shoulder with a thumb. "Back at Magruder's. She saw you leave but couldn't keep up when you took off like a rocket. I have my motorcycle now, so I followed. Took some time to get past the obstacles, but I finally made it."

I nodded toward my superhero invention. "Why did you take my stuff?"

"Thought you might need it." He nudged it with a shoe. "And seeing that your sister is as weak as a tadpole, I guessed right."

"You know what it does?"

"I'm not stupid, Eddie. I can see results, even if I have no clue how it works."

I took a step toward the unit, but Milligan snatched it up. "Not so fast, my young friend. I'll be glad to let you supercharge your sister again, but after that, I'm hanging on to it. Just show me how it works, and I'll let you borrow it. Then I'm going to sell it. Ninety percent of the cash goes to your mom, and I'll keep the rest for commission. Someone's gotta watch out for your family's finances."

Keeping my stare on Milligan, I slid my finger toward the projector's power switch. "This is no time to make a deal. Mephisto's trying to destroy Nirvana, and Sam and I are the only ones who can stop him."

"The only ones? I thought this little feud was between Mephisto and Damocles. Why are you two kids involved?"

I flipped the switch, but nothing appeared. Either the computer or the projector had run out of power. My legs trembled. I had to stay calm. But every option was terrible. If I zapped Sam again, she might die. If I didn't, a quake would kill us both. Or would it? I couldn't be sure exactly what damage the quake might do. I couldn't be sure of anything.

I looked at my watch — 3:41 a.m. If Mephisto kept his word, we had about nineteen minutes left. Trying to keep my voice calm, I raised a hand. "Listen, Milligan. Mephisto is about to zap the city with the biggest earthquake yet. We might have only a few minutes to get out of here or we'll be crushed by a million tons of rocks."

A slight tic twitched Milligan's lip. "Then I'd better be going." He turned and walked into the tunnel, my invention still in hand. "You'll follow if you know what's good for you."

"Wait!" I pulled Sam to her feet, but her legs buckled and she crumpled to the floor. I called out, "Milligan, you said you promised my mom —"

"That I'd find you." He pivoted toward us. "And I did. Now I'm putting pressure on you to leave this place. I'm not gonna carry you, and I'm not gonna beg." He turned again and walked into the tunnel, disappearing in the shadows.

I stuffed the projector and computer into my pack and knelt next to Sam. Lying on her back, she looked at me and whispered in a lamenting tone, "Eddie, I don't want to get crushed by a million tons of rocks."

"Don't worry. I'll get you out of here somehow." I detached my flashlight and pushed it into Sam's hands. "You're in charge of the light."

She gave me a weak grin. "Coolness."

After putting the backpack on, I slid one of my arms under her shoulders and the other under her legs. Grunting with the effort, I lifted her as I straightened. My arms shook. Either she was heavier than I remembered or I was weaker. Maybe both.

I staggered around the hole and into the tunnel. As darkness enfolded us, I whispered, "Shine the light just a step or two in front of us."

"Easy peasy." She pointed the beam at the tunnel floor exactly where I needed it.

"Perfect. Now stay as quiet as possible." As I walked, every muscle ached. The sound of cascading water echoed, making it impossible to tell how far away the exit was. Every footfall sent a shockwave up my leg, a constant reminder that an earthquake could strike at any second.

When we finally arrived at the waterfall, I leaned around it and whispered, "Sam, shine the light a few steps past the water.

She aimed the beam in that direction, illuminating my superhero invention balanced on a ledge in the gorge's wall, my spool line tied to the top handle. The line began lifting, taking my invention with it.

"I'll be back." I laid Sam down, leaped through the waterfall, and grabbed the handle. The line jerked, but I held on. As I began untying it, Milligan cursed from street level and called out, "Stop it,

Eddie. You can't carry that thing out of here. Let me do it."

"I don't trust you." I focused on my fingers while Sam's flashlight beam wavered and water dripped from my hair to my hands. When I finished untying the knot and released the line, the end dangled near the ground.

Milligan called again. "Now what're you gonna do? Climb the rope while carrying that gadget and your sister at the same time? Maybe I could pull you guys up one at a time, but you'll have to send the gadget before you come. Otherwise no one will be down there to tie it to the rope."

I fumed. Milligan didn't want to help us. He just wanted my invention. Once he got it, he would take off. "Don't worry about us. We'll get out of here without your help."

"If that's the way you feel about it. I guess I'll just have to find your mother and tell her you chose to get crushed to a pulp. She's sure to die of heartache." After a short pause, he added, "By the way, there's a hologram message floating in the air. It says the next earthquake is coming in twelve minutes and five seconds, and the numbers are counting down. It also says, 'Meet me in the Dead Zone, or else.'"

"The Dead Zone? Which part?"

"Beats me. I'm heading for Magruder's. I can get there in less than twelve minutes." Seconds later, a motorcycle engine revved a few times before fading.

I pulled the rope. It reeled down and collected in a pile at my feet.

The flashlight beam shone in my face. "Eddie?"

Sam said with a mournful tone. "What are we going to do? I don't want Mom to die of heartache."

I patted my belt and touched the one remaining spool. "Even if I could throw a claw to the top, attaching to something sturdy up there is a one-in-a-million chance. Then I'd have to carry you while climbing. We'd never make it in time."

Still holding the flashlight, Sam staggered straight through the pouring water and into my arms. As I held her up, she looked at me. "I heard what Damocles said about me maybe dying if you make me a superhero again." A tear spilled from her eye and joined the water streaming down her cheek. "If I have to die, I wanna die a superhero. A superhero like you."

I bit my lip. As I gazed into her fear-widened eyes, my own tears welled. "You're right. I guess it's our only chance."

She smiled. "Goody. Let's do it."

Moving quickly, I guided her to the dry side of the waterfall and set her on her bottom, then aimed my invention's lens at her. "I'm not sure how much power it has, but … here goes." I flipped the power switch on.

Once again bright light shot out and covered Sam with an X-ray wash. As usual, the power shut off on its own, but the exposure time seemed shorter than before. Maybe my mind was playing tricks with me.

Sam leaped up and flexed her swelling biceps. "I feel super. Even my ankles don't hurt anymore."

"Great." After reattaching the flashlight, I reeled

out my last spool line and attached the claw to her belt. "Now see if you can climb to the top."

She backed up, then sprinted toward the wall and jumped way over my head. Reaching with both hands, she grabbed a protruding pipe, swung up to a standing position on it, and jumped again, this time out of sight.

"I made it," she called from above.

"Okay, now attach the claw to the hydrant."

"All right." After a few seconds, she called down again. "Ready."

I stuffed the superhero device into the backpack and pushed the auto-reel button on the spool. The line tightened, and I zipped upward, pushing against the wall with my feet. When I reached the top, I scrambled over the edge and looked around.

Milligan was nowhere in sight. In the sky, huge lights spelled out 09:33, 09:32, 09:31. I hissed, "We have to get to the Dead Zone."

Sam detached the claw from the hydrant. "But shouldn't we tell Mom what's going on?"

"She'll be fine. Stopping that earthquake is more important." After reeling the rest of the line into the spool, I grabbed her bike and scanned the wheels, pedals, and chain. Nothing was bent or broken, but the seat couldn't possibly hold both of us. "How're we going to do this?" I asked.

Sam hopped onto the bike. "Get on my shoulders, and leave the rest to me."

"On your shoulders?"

"You're wasting time. Remember I'm Princess Queenie Unicorn —"

"Never mind." I set a foot on the back tire and vaulted up to her shoulders with my legs draped over her chest. "Comfortable?"

"No. You feel like a dizzy gorilla with a sharp butt bone."

I laughed. "Is my coccyx toxic?"

"What?"

"Forget it. Just go."

She wrapped an arm over my legs. "Which way?"

"Straight ahead for now. I'll guide you."

Sam pedaled furiously. The sudden surge made me lurch backwards, but her strong arm kept me from falling.

As we zipped along, I called out directions. The little squirt did everything right, from weaving around holes in the street, to hopping over curbs without a pause, to dodging sparking electrical wires. Princess Queenie was on the ball.

I shouted, "You're doing great. We really make a good team, don't we?"

"The best."

As she continued pumping the pedals, I kept glancing at the timer in the sky. It dropped under seven minutes, then five minutes, then three. We wheeled into the Dead Zone with one minute and twenty-eight seconds left on the clock.

"Sam, stop." When she did, I hopped off the bike and shouted, "Mephisto! Damocles is here! Stop the countdown!"

In the sky, the clock marched on — 01:20, 01:19, 01:18.

"He doesn't believe you," Sam said.

I shed my backpack, withdrew the superhero

device, and set it to the side, allowing me to reach the computer and projector. I had no way to recharge the batteries, but maybe …

With only moonlight to guide me, I set the projector unit down, detached the flashlight, and unscrewed the base. Two batteries slid into my hand. Jack had said the unit could use regular batteries, but were these the same size?

I glanced at the timer — 00:58, 00:57. "Sam, watch for bad guys while I try something." I knelt, opened the computer's power-source compartment, and replaced the batteries with the ones from the flashlight, then turned the unit on. But how long would they last? We had used the flashlight quite a bit.

"I see someone," Sam said, pointing. "No. Two someones. They're coming this way."

I straightened and looked. A pair of men sauntered toward us, hoods shadowing their faces. "Maybe Damocles can scare them off, but get ready to fight anyway."

The projector flashed Damocles's hologram. He looked around as if assessing the situation. I glanced at the timer — 00:40, 00:39. "Damocles, the big quake's going to hit in thirty-eight seconds. I already shouted for Mephisto, but he hasn't shown up."

When Damocles spotted the two men, he whispered, "Sam, you'll have to do the fighting. Just stay with me and do what I do. Eddie, send me at them and keep shouting for Mephisto to meet us. Got it?"

"Got it." I looked at the two men. They had stopped and stared at us. One drew a long knife.

Damocles whispered, "Now."

I guided his hologram toward the men and shouted, "Mephisto, Damocles is here!"

Damocles moved his arms and legs as if running. Sam dashed alongside him. When they reached the men, the one with the knife jabbed it through Damocles's image. Damocles threw a punch into his gut. Sam copied the motion and drilled her fist into his stomach, making him double over and collapse. Damocles kicked the second man in the groin while Sam leaped and did the same. He, too, crumpled in place.

While Sam and Damocles stood guard over the fallen thugs, I looked again at the timer, now down to fifteen seconds. I shouted at the top of my lungs. "Mephisto, stop the earthquake countdown! Damocles is here!"

The projector blinked off. Damocles disappeared. The batteries had died.

As the timer ticked under ten seconds, the thugs struggled to hands and knees and crawled away.

Sam backed toward me, still watching the thugs. "What do we do now, Eddie?"

When she arrived, I grasped her hand. Only eight seconds till the destruction of our home and all of Nirvana. "Just hang on tight. We'll get through this together."

CHAPTER 13

A Villain in a Chicken Suit?

When the timer ticked down to two seconds, it stopped. A voice rode the darkness. "A most intriguing demonstration."

Chet Graham stepped out from under a cluster of trees with a huge eagle perched on his shoulder. He held a projector similar to mine, its lens pointing toward a hologram at his side — a human that moved at his pace — Mephisto. Wearing a hawk-like cowl mask, complete with a hooked beak and huge feathered wings on his back, he looked ready to take off and fly.

Mephisto stood in a room with a window and grandfather clock against a wall behind him, and the entire room moved along with the hovering hologram. Several birds flitted about his head — parakeets, sparrows, and a crow, though he seemed to be ignoring them.

When Graham stopped a few paces away, Mephisto bowed in a formal manner. "Greetings, Eddie and Samantha Hertz."

My stomach threatened to upchuck everything inside, but I steeled myself and forced a confident nod. "Mephisto."

He looked around. "Where is Damocles? I saw him a moment ago when he dispatched the ruffians who threatened you."

"He's close by." I had no clue what else to say. To Mephisto, it probably looked like Damocles turned tail and ran while leaving two kids by themselves in the Dead Zone. "He knows what's going on."

"So he is employing children as his emissaries." Mephisto laughed in a scornful way. "Is he afraid to face me?"

I huffed. "Spoken by a hologram wearing a goofy chicken suit."

He laughed again. "Well struck, Eddie. It appears that I am dealing with a young man who possesses high intellect and a sharp wit."

"Don't sweet talk me, Mephisto." Hoping to keep my arms from shaking, I crossed them tightly over my chest. "Let's get to business. What do you want?"

"It's quite simple. Deliver one billion dollars in cash, and I will hand over the earthquake mechanism. While on the Stellar rooftop, I gave Damocles three days, but his delays and cowardice have shortened the time. Now he has twelve hours."

I glanced at my watch — 4:01 a.m.

"If he fails," Mephisto continued, "as I warned earlier, I will destroy Nirvana and set my sights on leveling every major city in the world, and the price to stop me will be ten billion dollars."

I glared at Chet Graham, trying to ignore the huge predator on his shoulder. "So you're working for Mephisto after all. You even have one of his birds as a playmate."

Graham batted at the eagle, making it hop to the ground in a flutter of its massive wings. Then, letting out an angry squawk, it flew back to his shoulder. "Mephisto sent this wretched eagle to keep an eye on me, and it insists on digging its claws into my skin to make sure I don't step out of line."

I huffed. "And you expect me to believe that lie?"

Graham shoved the eagle off again. This time it stayed on the ground. "Listen, Eddie, believe what you want; I'm just trying to keep Nirvana safe. I can't stop Mephisto, so I'm trying to help him get in touch with Damocles. If you'll deliver the message, tell him that I have contacts at banks, but they won't listen to me if I'm alone. We have to collect the money together. It's the only way."

I half closed an eye. "How much of the billion did Mephisto promise you?"

"Eddie, I assure you —"

"You cannot convince him, Mr. Graham," Mephisto said. "The evidence is against you, and he knows it. But, being as smart as he is, he also knows he must go along with your appeal. At the very least, he will contact Damocles and relay my demands. Give him the address, and we will be on our way."

Graham pulled a business card from his shirt pocket and extended it. "All phone systems are down, so Damocles will have to meet me in person at this location."

I took the card. Keeping my stare fixed on him, I slid it into my pants pocket. "I'll tell him."

"Thank you." Graham squinted at my projector unit. "Why have you been hauling that thing all across Nirvana?"

I picked it up and returned it to my backpack. "To keep criminals like you guessing."

"And what's this?" He reached for my superhero device, but I grabbed it just in time.

"It's none of your business."

Mephisto narrowed his eyes. "Considering Damocles's sudden disappearance, Mr. Graham, I am beginning to understand what's going on here. Get that device for me."

Graham lunged for it, but Sam jumped in front of me and punched him in the stomach. He flew back ten feet and smacked his head on the sidewalk. His projector fell from his limp hands and blinked off.

I ran to the projector, snatched it up, and hurried back to Sam. "Let's grab everything and get out of here."

After we pushed the projectors and the superhero device into my overstuffed backpack, she mounted her bike, I climbed onto her shoulders, and we rode out of the Dead Zone. From the rear, Graham shouted, "Follow them!"

I looked back. The shadow of an eagle closed in on us from above.

"Faster," I yelled. "To Magruder's."

"I know the way." Sam pumped her legs madly, making them blur. Like a two-wheeled rocket, we zipped along the sidewalk, again dodging holes and flying over ruts and ditches.

I searched for the eagle. It now flew far behind us. In the sky, a new digital clock appeared and began counting down from "11:56:00." A message below it read "Time until a quake comes that will destroy all of Nirvana. If Damocles isn't a coward, he will do what is right to save the city."

Soon, Magruder's came into sight, easily visible in the moon's glow. The bike slowed. Sam labored at the pedals, coughing.

I called out, "Stop!"

She toppled to the side with me still on her shoulders. We crashed to the sidewalk and rolled into the bordering lawn. I scrambled to all fours, crawled to her, and helped her rise to her knees. She vomited, spewing half-digested meatball chunks and bread across the grass.

I patted her back. "Let me know when you're ready, and I'll help you get to Magruder's. We'll find some water there."

She collapsed and face planted in the turf.

"Sam!" I pulled her limp body into my lap and cleared dirt from her mouth. She gasped shallow breaths, no sign of anything blocking her throat. As I stood, I lifted her and staggered toward Magruder's.

I sneaked a peek at the sky. The eagle flew in a circle about fifty feet overhead. By the time I closed in on the front door, my arms ached. I could barely walk. I probably looked like a kid zombie carrying an unconscious victim, ready to feast on her brains. But I didn't care. I had to help Sam.

The door flew open, and two men charged out. One took Sam and dashed into the restaurant, while the other held my arm, whispering, "Let's get you inside."

Half dazed, I let him lead me through the door. He set me on a chair. Nearby, the first man laid Sam on the carpet, pushed a folded apron under her head, and elevated her legs over his, while the second man hurried toward the kitchen, calling, "I'll get water, Doctor."

"Doctor?" I repeated to the first man. "Are you a doctor?"

He nodded as he held Sam's wrist and looked at his watch. Shaved bald and pale, his head looked like a misshapen cue ball. "I'm Doctor Ross. What's your name?"

"Eddie Hertz."

He blinked. "What hurts?"

"My name is Hertz. But never mind about me. Is Sam all right?"

"Sam? I thought she was a girl." Dr. Ross shook his head. "Sometimes hard to tell these days, especially when they're this young."

"She *is* a girl. Samantha Hertz." My bladder sent a sudden all-full signal. The tension and running around had taken its toll. "Just check her out while I go to the bathroom, okay?"

"Of course."

I ran to the men's room. The toilet in the stall had split in half, and water flooded the floor, though nothing spewed. The urinal on the wall, however, seemed fine. After relieving myself there, I dashed back to Sam and the doctor.

"How is she?"

"Heart rate and respiration are elevated. No fever." Dr. Ross looked at me. "What happened? She's as pale as a ghost."

"Just worn out, I think. We got chased by some guys in the Dead Zone."

He brushed dirt from Sam's cheek with a napkin. "Scared half to death, I suppose. She might be in shock."

I glanced around. The restaurant was nearly empty — just one waitress mopping spills and the two guys who helped us. Candles burned at some of the tables, casting undulating light across the dim room.

"I'm back." The other man returned with a glass of water. He looked familiar, maybe Victor, the manager Mom mentioned so many times. "Doctor Ross, this boy's mother is one of the waitresses here. She went out looking for these two kids a while ago."

"Mom went by herself?" I asked. "But the city's getting more dangerous every minute."

Victor shook his head. "A man went with her. He seemed like a tough guy, and she knew him, so I thought she'd be all right."

A shudder ran up my spine. "Was the guy's name Milligan?"

"I don't know. He said something about seeing you two near the Stellar. They're heading that way." Victor crouched near Sam with the glass in hand. "Sorry it took so long. We don't have any water pressure, so I melted some ice over a candle. Burned my hand while doing it."

While Dr. Ross held Sam's head up, Victor set the glass at her lips and helped her drink. She slurped and swallowed, apparently awake enough to handle it.

"What happened to all the people who were here before?" I asked.

Victor nodded toward the ceiling. "The message in the sky says less than twelve hours to the big one, so people took off, trying to get out of town. With all the streets looking like a war zone, it could take a long time to leave, if it's even possible. Besides, the last quake split my restaurant's foundation and collapsed half of the roof. This place wouldn't last through a blow from the big bad wolf, much less another earthquake."

"Is it safe to stay here for a while?"

"For the moment. But we'd better be long gone when the next quake comes."

"She's had enough." Dr. Ross took the water glass and set it on the floor. "Could she have touched a downed power line?"

I shook my head. "Like I said, I think it's just exhaustion. And she threw up."

"Not good. Not good at all." Dr. Ross patted Sam's cheek. "Samantha, can you hear me?"

Her eyes fluttered open. They flared in fear until she caught sight of me. "Eddie? Where are we?"

I knelt next to her. "At Magruder's."

Her eyes darted. "Where's Mom?"

"She went looking for us."

Her cheeks flushed red. "We have to find her before Milligan makes her die of heartache!"

Dr. Ross squinted at me. "Is she prone to vivid dreams? Hallucinations?"

"Uh … yeah. She believes in fairies."

Sam gave me a death stare. "Eddie, you heard what Milligan said."

"Sure, Sam. We'll find her." I detached the flashlight from my belt. "Victor, do you have fresh batteries around? My flashlight's dead."

"Yep." He shot to his feet and hurried toward the kitchen again.

"If you're heading out to look for your mom," Dr. Ross said, "we'll take good care of Samantha."

Sam grabbed my wrist tightly. "You can't go without me. You know that."

I gazed into her determined eyes. Of course she meant that I needed her as Princess Queenie, but I couldn't risk her getting even sicker. I had to figure out a way to keep her here. "Dr. Ross, would you check Sam's ankles? She fell a couple of times."

"Of course." He reached for a nearby candle and set it close on the floor, then slid her pant legs up and ran gentle fingers along her skin. The bruises were still there, though they had faded quite a bit. "Could be a hairline compression fracture."

"So should she try to walk?"

He shook his head. "She should rest until we have a chance to X-ray both legs."

"Then there's no way she can go with me, right?"

He laughed under his breath. "If it were up to me, she would be at the emergency room. But we don't even have a working triage station anymore. The last shake knocked everything down. I was about to head over there to help the workers set it back up when you came."

Sam crossed her arms. "Then go help them. I'm going with Eddie."

"No, young lady. If you try to walk —"

"Got 'em Eddie," Victor said as he hustled back. He handed me four batteries. "Will that be enough?"

"Perfect." I popped two into the flashlight and slid the other pair into my pocket. "I'm going to take a quick look outside. See if my mom's around."

As I straightened, Sam's eyes widened again. "Eddie, you can't talk to Damocles without me!"

"Damocles?" Dr. Ross laid a hand on her forehead. "Maybe she's feverish after all."

Sam's cheeks flushed even redder. "Let me up. I want to get up right now."

Dr. Ross and Victor helped her to a booth seat. When she sat, she looked at me with imploring eyes. "I can go with you if you'll get me a wheelchair. You don't even have to push me. I'll wheel it myself."

"I can get you a wheelchair," Dr. Ross said, "but you're staying here."

Sam's bottom lip quivered. "Eddie. Don't leave me behind. We're a team. Remember?"

My own words came back to haunt me. I had said that. And it was true. She had been amazingly brave and smart. "You're right, Sam." I turned to Dr. Ross. "Do you mind getting the wheelchair?"

"Not at all. I'll pick up a stethoscope and a blood pressure cuff, and I'll bring a nurse, too. We'll check her more thoroughly." He turned and headed for the door.

With Victor looking on, I grasped Sam's hand.

"I'll go outside for a few minutes and check the area. See if Mom's nearby. I'll be back soon. I promise."

"Just long enough to talk to Damocles, right?"

I glanced at Victor and gave him a wink to avoid explaining what she meant. "Right. No longer than that. I won't go anywhere else without you."

Victor patted me on the back. "No worries, Eddie. We'll take good care of Sam."

"Thanks." With my backpack on and my flashlight in hand, I marched toward the restaurant exit.

"I'm trusting you, Eddie," Sam called with a plaintive voice. "We're a team."

"I know" was all I could say as I hurried out the door.

CHAPTER 14

When Two Holograms Argue, Is It Really an Argument?

Once I arrived in the restaurant's parking lot, I flicked on the flashlight and aimed the beam toward the collapsed triage area. At least a dozen people scurried about hammering tent pegs into the ground, dragging generators from one spot to another, and putting up light standards, but Mom was nowhere in sight.

I walked to the rear of the restaurant, slid my backpack to the ground, and sat against a brick wall near a head-high dumpster. With the top lid open, it smelled like rotten eggs and sour milk, but at least no one was around, not even Graham's eagle.

Breathing through my mouth to avoid the stench, I withdrew the projector and put the two extra batteries into it. I aimed the lens away from the wall and turned the unit on. Within seconds, Damocles appeared. When he saw me, he removed his mask and sat in front of me, his dreadlocks swaying around his concerned face. "Where are we, Eddie?"

I touched the wall. "Behind Magruder's restaurant, where my mom works."

"Where's Sam?"

"Inside with the manager. A doctor went to get some stuff so he can examine her. She got sick."

"I assume she's reacting to getting supercharged with your invention again."

Averting my eyes, I nodded.

"How many times have you charged her up?"

"Three."

"Is this the sickest she's been?"

"I think so. She heaved her guts this time." I gave him a quick summary of Mephisto's latest demands and a few details about our escape, including the fact that I was able to take Graham's hologram projector.

Damocles looked at the countdown timer in the sky. "Is his projector combined with a computer, like yours?

"I think so." I fished it out of the backpack and looked it over. It appeared to be similar to mine, a newer model that combined the computer and projector into an interlocked unit. "I'll turn it on."

I flipped the switch. A new hologram took shape next to Damocles — Mephisto in his winged-chicken-thing costume, standing near the grandfather clock in the same room as before. A canary flew past from right to left, then a green parrot in the opposite direction. When he saw me, he scowled and looked around. Then he turned toward Damocles. His eyes widened, and he backed up a step.

I glanced at the two computers. Their cameras rotated in all directions, obviously building a virtual reality environment for each man, though Mephisto seemed unable to tell that Damocles was merely a hologram. Maybe his projector couldn't see mine.

Mephisto sneered. "Well, I see that Damocles has decided to stop hiding behind a pair of children."

Damocles bowed his head. "And I see that you're still showing the entire world what a coward is really like — murdering innocent people, blackmailing the world to fill your pockets with loot, and masquerading as a half-plucked hen."

Mephisto looked at his outfit. "I'm a falcon, a skilled and swift predator."

Damocles growled. "You're a fowl fiend, a feathered fool, and fox food. And I'm the fox."

Mephisto set a fist on his hip. "Insults and threats won't stop me, Damocles. You have less than twelve hours to deliver one billion dollars to the address Chet Graham gave to your young friend. He will meet you there."

I sucked in a breath. The address. I forgot all about it. I pulled the card from my pocket and read it out loud. "Thirteen-thirteen Snakepit Gulley in Mosquito Lagoon." I looked at Damocles. "Isn't that a few miles outside of Nirvana?"

"It is." Damocles glared at Mephisto. "You were leading two children into a snake-infested swamp?"

"The swamp is merely a barrier that protects an old hideout of mine. Once you get past the cottonmouths, the rest of the way is easy."

I concealed a tight swallow. Cottonmouths? I took in a deep breath and exhaled slowly. I could do that. For the sake of Nirvana, I'd face any danger. Except maybe scorpions.

Damocles gave Mephisto a sharp stare. "Do you still have scorpions in the swamp?"

"I assume there are still many thousands of them, maybe millions by now, but they stay hidden most of the time. Too much noise will bring them out in a deadly swarm, so you will have to proceed across the swamp in complete silence."

I swallowed again. Scorpions. Why did it have to be scorpions?

Damocles half closed an eye. "So Graham will meet us there and not you."

"Correct. That is an unsavory place, so I never go there anymore. I will be elsewhere, safe from the coming earthquake."

"You do realize," Damocles said, "that we can find your location by looking up the transmission address on your projection unit."

"Of course I realize that. I was just about to leave when your signal came in."

Damocles crossed his arms in front, making his massive biceps bulge. "Very well. Then leave. We won't be able to follow you."

"Leave?" Mephisto blinked. "Do you mean right now? At this moment?"

"Yes. Right now."

Mephisto glanced left and right, as if confused. I stared at Damocles and his confident stance. He acted like he was calling a bluff, seeing if Mephisto really intended to leave.

Mephisto straightened and squared his shoulders. "I will depart at the time of my own choosing."

"That's fine," Damocles said, his arms still crossed. "We'll just leave your unit on and follow the transmission address until we find you."

"Not if I stop the transmission." As Mephisto stayed in his defiant stance, his hologram faded until it vanished.

Damocles turned toward me. "Do you know how to find that computer's transmission log and translate its origin codes?"

"I think so. It's a newer model, so I can't be sure."

"If you can't, you'll have to go to thirteen-thirteen Snakepit Gulley and face the venomous snakes in the swamp."

"And the scorpions." I looked at the unit's tiny screen — a touch-sensitive display with menu selections. "I'll see what I can do."

"Have you tried using Mastix lately?"

I shook my head. "Having it fail every time got kind of discouraging."

"Let's multi-task." Damocles drew the holographic Mastix from his belt. The thongs instantly flashed with shimmering light. "While you're tracking down the address, I'll teach you how to use Mastix, assuming it ever recognizes you as a superhero and starts working."

"That's a big assumption. But all right."

While I clicked through the computer's menus, Damocles demonstrated how to use Mastix as a weapon, including collecting deadly projectiles in its thongs, creating a web of electricity that can capture a villain, shooting hundreds of paralyzing sparks in a 180-degree arc, and combining the sparks in a single super-powered lightning bolt. With the final ability, a blinding bolt of light blasted from his phantom Mastix and disappeared the moment it rocketed past the hologram's boundary.

When he finished, he refastened Mastix to his belt. "That's all. Any questions?"

"None that I can think of." I looked at the real Mastix as it lay dark inside my backpack. Actually I did have a huge question. Would it ever decide to see me as a superhero? But Damocles probably couldn't answer that.

"Did you find the address?" he asked.

"The computer's tracing the codes now." After a few seconds, an address appeared on the screen. "It's thirteen-thirteen Snakepit Gulley. The same as on the card."

"So he was lying about his location. And probably about a lot more."

"Like what?"

"Allow me to process my thoughts for a while. The ramifications are huge, and I have to make sure I'm right."

"Okay, but what do I do?"

"Go to thirteen-thirteen Snakepit Gulley and cross the swamp, as planned."

"Uh … sure … yeah. That's easy to say."

"Are you afraid of snakes?"

"Not really. I can face them."

"Then what's wrong?"

"Well, I don't have a billion dollars. If I show up without the money, he'll go through with the earthquake, not to mention that he'll probably kill me."

"Right. Without Sam, you're pretty defenseless."

Warmth rushed into my cheeks, and guilt punched my gut hard. "I can't charge her up again, Damocles. She'll get sicker. She might even die."

Damocles's tone softened to the kind adults use when they're trying to help a kid make a mature decision that most kids would never have to make. "You can't be certain of that, Eddie. She's always recovered before."

"But I can't risk her life. She's my sister."

"If the big quake comes, everyone in the city will die, including Sam."

I nodded slowly. "So Sam could die either way."

Damocles walked closer and crouched within reach. "Superheroes often have to make decisions like this. We call it a moral dilemma. Will you sacrifice one person to save millions? Or will you save one person and hope that decision doesn't lead to the death of millions? A real superhero has to figure out a way to solve both problems."

I looked up at him, tears flooding my eyes. "You're a superhero, Damocles. What would you do if you were me?"

"If I tell you, I don't think you'll ever become a superhero."

"Because I have to figure it out myself?"

He nodded. "The decision has to come from your heart, not mine. And even if I told you what to do, you might not be able to do it. My idea might not work. Obviously I've made mistakes before. Otherwise, I wouldn't be dead, and you wouldn't have to deal with this dilemma. That's my fault."

He sat, floating an inch off the ground, and laid a hand on my knee, though it couldn't make physical contact. "Eddie, Nirvana needs someone who'll try to stop an earthquake. But they need more than that. Sure, if I tell you what to do, maybe you'll stop the quake and save Nirvana and your sister. You'd be a hero for a day. But what Nirvana really needs is a superhero who is still a superhero tomorrow, and the next day, and the next. Mephisto or someone like him will try again to kill innocent people, but I can't keep advising you forever. Nirvana needs a superhero who will last. Nirvana needs you."

I brushed a tear from each eye. "Why can't you advise me? I can get new batteries for years."

"Because the essence I put into that wallet can't be recharged. It will eventually die. The more times you project my hologram and the more time I spend with you, the faster it will run out. My guess is we have ten minutes left to spend together."

"Ten minutes?" My throat pinched, pitching my voice higher. "I can't do this without you."

"You have to. I created this solution to my death for this very purpose, to train a replacement."

"But I'm no superhero. I'm just a kid. You need someone bigger and stronger. Not some weenie-armed little runt like me."

"Eddie, being a superhero isn't a matter of how big your arms are." He set his phantom hand on my chest. "It's how big your heart is. And you have the biggest heart I have ever seen."

My breaths grew shallow. I had the biggest heart? Was he confusing me with someone else? How could he think my heart was big?

As Damocles drew back, static ran across his hologram. His fingertips dissolved, turning to sparkling dust and dispersing. The disintegration progressed to his hands and continued up toward his forearms.

"Damocles?" My voice squeaked. "What's happening to you?"

He looked at his arm as it crumbled to sparks, his expression calm. "It looks like I overestimated my remaining time. I think I will be gone in seconds."

"No, Damocles! No!"

When I reached for the projector, he called out, "It's no use, Eddie." Now both of his arms were gone, and the dissolving line ran up his thighs as he floated in midair. "Even if you turn off the projector, I will keep dissolving. Nothing can stop it now."

More heat surged into my cheeks. Tears spilled and trickled to my chin. "At least tell me what you were thinking about Mephisto. I mean, what else was he lying about?"

Now the dissolving line raced up his torso. Only his head and chest remained. "Listen carefully. Since Mephisto was transmitting from the Snakepit address, it means that place isn't an old hideout. It's where he is and always has been. He was a hologram on the Stellar roof and in the Dead Zone. In all of my years battling against his evil deeds, I have never met him face to face."

Damocles's head now floated by itself, his chin dissolving. "I think he never leaves his hideout. For some reason he's either trapped there or he doesn't really —"

His mouth fractured along with his voice, leaving only the area above his nose. His glimmering eyes looked so sincere, so passionate. The moment a tear spilled from each one, his remains exploded in a silent splash of sparks.

Twinkling like fairy dust, the sparks rained toward the ground. I tried to catch some in my hand, but they passed through and disappeared.

The sensation brought Sam's fantasies to mind, her hopes and dreams about her own heroes, caught in the sparkling whirlwind of her vivid imagination's idea of the fairy princess she longed to be.

I closed my fist over the last vanishing spark and whispered, "Fairies really do exist."

My vision blurred by tears, I grabbed Graham's projector and heaved it into the dumpster. It squished on something soft before striking bottom with a metallic clank. Then I picked up my computer/projection combo and, with a guttural shout, flung it into the dumpster. It hit bottom right away with a loud clatter.

My backpack lay on the ground. I removed Mastix, still dark from the handle to the end of its thongs, and fastened it to my belt. Only the superhero device remained inside. I grabbed the strap and lifted the pack. I couldn't let Sam go through so much suffering again. My invention would have to join the trash heap.

I slung the backpack toward the top of the dumpster and watched it sail. Just as it reached the peak of its arc, Graham's eagle swooped down, snatched it in its claws, and lifted into the sky, the pack dangling. Within seconds, it was gone.

My mouth dropped open. What had I done? Now Mephisto would have the superhero device. How would he use it? Knowing him, he would figure out how to make it more powerful than ever.

Heaving deep breaths, I leaned against the wall and stared down at my shoes. Tears dripped to the laces. A sob welled up. I tried to hold it back, but it burst out in a gut-wrenching spasm.

My back against the bricks, I slid down to a crouch with my hands over my face and cried. Hard. Damocles, my hero, was gone forever. And now Nirvana would never again have a superhero to keep it safe.

CHAPTER 15

Do I Really Have to Save a Scoundrel?

"Eddie?"

I looked toward the sound — a man's voice. Familiar.

A dim, moon-cast shadow drew closer. Milligan stepped into view from around the dumpster. "Here you are. I thought I heard someone shout."

As I rose, I stealthily brushed tears with my knuckles. "What do you want?"

"Just looking for you. Your mom and I couldn't find you in that hole in the street, so we came back to the restaurant." He leaned to the side and looked toward the front of the building. "I found him."

A wheelchair appeared from around the corner, Sam in the seat with her ankles bandaged and taped, pushed by Dr. Ross. A woman wearing dark blue scrubs followed. Sam grinned. "See? I knew he wouldn't leave without me."

"You were right," Dr. Ross said. "I'm sorry I doubted you."

When they all arrived, I looked behind them. No one else followed. "Where's Mom?"

Milligan jerked his thumb toward the street. "She

went back to your apartment looking for you. I said I'd stick around here in case you showed up."

Sam tugged on my wrist. "I saw her out the window. I waved, but she didn't see me. By the time I wheeled myself out there, she was gone. That's when Milligan saw me, and he started looking for you. I knew you wouldn't leave me, so I asked Victor to get some food for our next adventure." She glanced around. "Did you talk to Damocles?"

I looked straight at Sam. Her eyes, just like Damocles's, gleamed with sincerity. It was time to stop hiding the truth from the adults. "Yes, I talked to him. I know what we have to do."

"Together?" she asked, her eyes hopeful.

"Together. Always. I'm not going to let anything break up our team."

She lifted a hand. "Princess Power Pledge."

I slapped her palm and tried to burp, but it sounded more like squishing a bloated caterpillar, two out of ten on a burp scale. Hers was deep and resonate, definitely nine plus.

Dr. Ross turned to the woman in scrubs. "Mabel, what do you think?"

The woman nodded. "I think she can go, but no walking allowed."

"Agreed." Dr. Ross shifted back toward me. "Are you going home to see your mom? She's sick with worry."

"Can a wheelchair get through?" I asked.

Milligan shook his head. "Not on your normal path. Word on the street says the only solid pavement that goes that far is in the Dead Zone. I'd better come along."

I blew out a heavy sigh. "Listen. We've walked and biked all over town tonight, including the Dead Zone, and we've been fine. We can make it home without you watching over us."

"I'm here," Victor said as he jogged around the building. He set two brown paper bags next to Sam in the chair. "A sandwich and bottle of water for each of you."

I gave him a thankful nod. "That's super." I hustled to the back of the wheelchair and grabbed the handles. "Need to use the restroom before we go, Sam?"

"Nope. Already went. Mabel helped me."

"Great." I pushed her toward the walkway leading to the Dead Zone. "Thanks for everything, Victor, Dr. Ross, and Mabel."

"No, you don't, Eddie," Milligan called from behind me. "I'm coming with you."

I tried to push faster, but between the chair's weight and having to dodge some deep cracks in the pavement, it was no use. Within a few seconds, Milligan caught up and walked at my side. "Where's that machine that turns your sister into Supergirl?"

I scowled. "As if I'd tell you."

"Just thought you might use it. Heal her ankles. Make her feel better. That's what good brothers do."

"Give me a break. What do you know about being a good brother?"

"I'm being a good brother to your mom right now. Watching over you."

"Like you did when you took my invention?" I blinked at him. "Wait a minute. You're not my mother's brother."

Milligan slid a hand into his pocket. "Obviously your mom never told you about me. I'm her half brother. We have the same father. After my mother died, he got married to your grandma, and they had your mom."

"So you're my uncle?"

"Sort of. Half-uncle, I guess."

"Well, you tried to steal my invention, so you've got nothing to say to me about being a brother." I picked up my pace toward the Dead Zone, leaning harder as I pushed the wheelchair.

Milligan caught up and strode again at my side. "I was just trying to convince you to leave that hole before you got killed."

"Don't try to con me. I'm not stupid."

"Look, I know you don't trust me. And I'm no angel, that's for sure, but I promised your mom I'd look after you. And I'm gonna do that. That's what a brother does. He looks after his sister, right?"

His words dug deep. He really knew how to strike at my heart. "So I'm supposed to believe you were really going to give her most of the money? That's bogus."

"But it's true. You invention is worth millions. Billions. I was hoping you'd help me turn it into a franchise, you know, pay us a million bucks to be a superhero for a day. Maybe we could form a partnership. You'd be the president and call the shots, and

I'd be the head of marketing. I could put together a promo video that would —"

"Just shut up, Milligan. I wouldn't trust you to obey the law of gravity." I wheeled Sam through the Dead Zone entry gate and turned toward our apartment building. Mosquito Lagoon lay beyond it, so we had to go that way no matter what.

"I figured you'd say that, Eddie, so I'll just be patient. No hurry, right? Maybe when you see I'm not the crook you think I am, you'll change your mind. I can wait."

As I hustled through the darkness of the Dead Zone, wary of every shifting shadow, I thought back to what he said the first time I met this liar. *Like father, like son. A do-gooder who thinks he's too high and mighty to work with someone like me. If you don't watch out, you'll meet the same fate. Trust me. I know what happens to people who don't play the game.*

"Tell you what," I said. "If you'll come clean and tell me what you know about my father, I'll let you know where my superhero invention is. No lies. I want proof."

Milligan shrugged. "There's not much to say, and I got no proof."

"Then just tell me what you know. I'll decide if I believe you or not."

"All right. The truth." He stayed quiet for a moment, the only sound the swishing of his jeans. "Here's the scoop. I wanted your dad to join me in my business, selling merchandise for some quick cash. But he was a lot like you. Clean as a whistle. Wouldn't even cross a street without the green light, if you know what I mean. Drove me nuts. He even turned me in for cashing in on some jewelry, claiming I was fencing for a burglary ring. Which was true, it turned out. I didn't know it till later.

"Anyway, one day your dad was coming home from a business trip, driving down highway two-fifty-two. You know, the one that curves real sharp at the river? Well, his brakes went out, and he flew off the road, right into the drink."

Milligan made a splash sound. "The current took him away, and he drowned. End of story."

I let the imagined scene soak in for a moment before responding. "Did anyone find the car? Check it for tampering?"

"Yep. Cops dragged it out. Someone cut the brake line. Had to be the head of the burglary ring, a mob boss, but he skipped town. Never heard from him again. The records are public. I'm surprised you never checked them."

"And you had an alibi?"

"Iron clad. In fact, I was with your mom. She was sick, and your dad was hurrying home to be with her, like the good husband he always was."

I nodded. "And Sam and I were gone to summer camp. That's why I didn't see you."

The sound of Sam's gentle whimpering rose from the chair.

"We'd better change the subject," I said.

"No problem. Just so you believe I'm telling the truth. I did hold a grudge against your dad, but I'm no murderer."

I pushed on in silence. Now that the conversation

had ended, exhaustion took hold and stretched my mouth into a yawn. When was the last time I slept? I looked up. The quake countdown had dropped to 10:48:15. Maybe I had time to go home and catch a nap, just a couple of hours, but then I might run into Mom. She'd never let me go to Mephisto's hideout.

Ahead, the gate that marked the exit to the Dead Zone loomed closer in the waning moonlight. Beyond it, people streamed along the sidewalk and street, heading for the city limits, some on bicycles, others jogging while lugging suitcases or towing carts and wagons loaded with stuff. Some hauled small children buckled in shoulder-mounted baby carriers.

Since dawn would soon break, they probably hoped to leave the moment the sun provided enough light. With cars clogging the pathways, pavement ripped up, and light poles leaning here and there, held in place by sparking electric wires, the people had to dodge about in lines that snaked around the obstacles.

I sighed. They were scared. As they should be. Even if they managed to get far enough away from the city to avoid getting killed, they would return to nothing but rubble. Homeless. And how could they possibly know how far to run in the first place?

I rolled my hand into a fist. I had to help them somehow. Be their superhero, like Damocles said. But how?

Mephisto and Graham probably hoped I would work with Damocles to get the ransom money, so they wouldn't expect me to show up at the Snakepit address for quite a while. Maybe it would be best to sneak over there before they were ready. That might be my only chance. Getting some rest would have to wait.

"Eddie," Milligan hissed. "Kick it in gear."

I looked back. Three men ran toward us, two with knives drawn. I pushed harder, driving my feet into a quick jog, but I couldn't possibly outrun these muggers, not while pushing a wheelchair.

Milligan ran alongside, constantly glancing behind us. "We'll never make it, Eddie." He pulled out a switchblade and snapped it open. "Just keep going and don't look back."

When he halted, I ran ahead, but I did look back. He raised his knife and dove into the trio, slicing with the blade. Whipping arms, thrashing bodies, and gleaming blades blurred. As I drew farther away, darkness shrouded the fight.

I swallowed hard. If only I could be a superhero now, I could squash those creeps. Milligan was a low-class thug, but I couldn't just let them cut him to pieces.

I stopped at the gate and touched Mastix at my belt. It stayed dark, but I still had my razor-disk pistol. "Sam, wheel yourself out to the crowds. I have to help Milligan."

CHAPTER 16

Sometimes You Just Have to Tell Mom.

"Eddie," Sam said, "you can't —"

"Just do it!" I shouted. "Don't argue!"

"All right. If you say so."

I ran toward the fight, detaching the pistol on the fly. Ahead, the three attackers huddled around Milligan, pummeling him with their fists as he lay on the ground. When I came within a few steps, I stopped and fired a disk at a mugger. *Pop.* The spinning razor buzzed into his face. He yelped and scampered away, trying to dig the disk out of his cheek.

I squeezed the trigger again. *Pop.* I hit another mugger in the back of the head. He howled and ran into the darkness. Just as I aimed at the third man, he staggered back, clutching the handle of Milligan's knife, the blade embedded in his stomach.

As he stumbled away, I reattached the pistol and knelt next to Milligan. Early morning light revealed bloody slashes across his forehead and cheeks as well as a black eye and a bruised jaw.

His lips barely moved as he whispered, "Whatever you did to those guys … thanks."

"You're welcome." I grabbed his wrist and pulled him to a sitting position. "Think you can stand?"

"Maybe."

Bracing my feet, I hauled him up. He wobbled but stayed upright as he dabbed at one of the facial cuts. "What did you shoot them with?"

"Razor disks." I glanced around. "Let's go before more muggers show up."

He limped toward the gate, grimacing with every step. "Don't wait for me. Just go on home. I'll be all right."

"You gotta be kidding." I grabbed his arm. "I'm not leaving you behind."

He stopped and pulled me to a halt. "Eddie. Listen. I'll come clean. Probably the first time in my life."

"All right." I looked into his eyes. They seemed sincere. "Spill it."

"I …" He pushed his hands into his pockets. "I didn't cut your dad's brake lines, but I did tell the mob boss where to find his car. He threatened to kill me if I didn't, but that's no excuse." He dragged the toe of a shoe across the walkway. "I guess I just wanted to save my own skin."

Rage boiling in my gut, I spoke through clenched teeth. "So why are you telling me now?"

His shoulders sagged. "Because you deserve the truth. Your dad was a better man than me. And you're just like him. I mean, you risked your life to save me, and you didn't have to." He took off his baseball cap and wadded it in his wringing hands. "I'm sorry for what I did. Really."

The fire inside burned on. A scream begged to erupt. My fists tightened into balls of fury. I wanted to punch him in the face. Break his nose. Make him suffer. Pay him back for what he did to me. To Sam. To Mom. He fractured our family. Shattered us into a million pieces. And we were still trying to glue them together.

"Here." Milligan leaned over and pointed at his nose. "Right here. As hard as you can. A bunch of times if you want. I deserve it."

Tears trickled down my cheeks. A new sob shook my body in a hard spasm. I raised my trembling fist and took aim.

Milligan closed his eyes, a new tic making the edges of his lids flinch. It would feel so good to land a punch. Just one good, hard one. But if I did, what would that make me? I wouldn't be like my dad — a better man, like Milligan said. I would just be an angry kid getting revenge. Hitting him wouldn't bring Dad home.

Breathing fast and shallow, I uncoiled my fist and lowered it. The fire in my gut died down, though the embers stayed hot. "I'm not going to hit you, Milligan."

He opened his eyes, relief obvious in his expression. "Tell you what. Let's go to your place. Find your mom. I'll talk to her. Tell her the truth." His brow lifted as he looked toward the gate. "Hey. Some guy is with Sam. You'd better check it out."

I spun that way. In the crowd of hustling people, Sam's wheelchair wasn't in sight. I ran toward the gate as fast as I could. When I arrived, I found Sam petting a cat sitting on her lap. No man stood anywhere nearby.

Spinning again, I looked into the Dead Zone. Milligan was gone. Mentioning Sam was a diversion.

"See the nice kitty?" As the gray tabby rubbed against Sam's chest, she petted it with long strokes. "Listen. He's purring."

I checked the cat's collar. No engraved name or tags. "Yeah. Probably lost. He's glad to find someone who cares."

"He's right. I care."

I gave the cat a long stroke of my own. "You do, Sam. You're as sweet as they come."

"Can we keep him?" she asked, her hands folded in a begging pose.

"Let's give him a little test." I gathered the cat and transferred him to the hood of a car just a step away. He immediately leaped back into Sam's lap. "All right. If Mom agrees, we'll keep him."

"Goody."

"Hang on. We have to go." I grabbed the wheelchair handles and pushed her into one of the long, snaking lines.

"Are we going home?"

"We'll pass by our building." A woman pushing a shopping cart filled with canned food cut in front of us, slowing our progress. "We can't stay, though."

"Don't we have to let Mom know we're okay?"

"One way or another." I broke out of the line, squeezed between two stalled cars, and wheeled into the street, weaving around other cars. It wasn't easy, but it was faster than the other way. "We'll stop and leave a note if we can. Maybe with Barney. But we have to keep going."

"Together. We're a team. And now we're three. I decided to name him Prince Edward Thomas Oscar Stephen Horsey O'Ryan. I picked Edward, 'cause that's your real name."

I laughed. "Thanks. I'll call him Petosho."

"You'd better not. He won't like it."

"Whatever." After a few more minutes of weaving, our apartment building came into sight. Barney sat with his back against a support column, one of four that used to hold up the portico. With the rifle in his lap and his eyes blinking, he looked like a weary soldier ready to fall asleep. The people hurrying by didn't seem to notice or care that he had a gun.

When he saw us drawing close, his head lifted. "So there you are."

I stopped the wheelchair in front of him. "Have you seen our mom?"

"Sure did. She's riding her bike around searching for you guys, and she stops to check with me to see if I've seen you. Kind of like a moon orbiting a planet." His brow furrowed. "But I guess a moon doesn't stop to talk to the planet, does it?'

"When is she due to come around again?"

Barney checked a watch on his wrist. "Maybe five minutes." He looked at the wheelchair. "What happened to Sam?"

"She fell. She's all right, though. Sprained ankles, we think."

Barney nodded. "Not used to the new bicycle. Takes some practice."

I looked at the building. Our section still seemed pretty much intact. If I could search around, I might find something to help us cross the swamp. "Is it safe to go to our apartment and get some stuff?"

"Probably. Your wing's pretty stable. Just use the north stairway, though. The south one's half gone."

"Great. Do you mind watching Sam while I'm up there?"

"Not a problem."

I parked the wheelchair next to Barney, snatched the flashlight from my belt, and ran into the building. After turning on the beam and hustling up the north stairs, I arrived at our apartment and entered through the open doorway.

Stepping lightly, I aimed the beam straight ahead, walked into my room, and looked around. Nothing useful caught my eye, just bedding, clothes, and my computer. What would help us get through a swamp? A boat? But what could we use as a boat?

I looked at my bed. An air mattress, maybe? Didn't we have a couple of those when we camped in the park with Dad?

I hurried to a hall closet and pulled stuff down from the top shelf — shoes, an umbrella, a golf club, a folded pup tent ... now I was getting closer ... a propane lantern, and ... yes ... a folded air mattress.

With the beam shining on the mattress, a quick scan revealed that it had a battery-operated internal motor that would make it self inflate. No problem. Even though I lost two batteries when I threw the projector in the dumpster, I could use the batteries in the flashlight if the ones in the motor didn't work.

After retrieving my old backpack from my room, I tucked Mastix inside. It would be best to keep it hidden from now on. If Mephisto saw it, he would figure out that Damocles had died. Besides, it didn't work for me. Maybe it never would.

I added the mattress to the backpack, put it on, and hurried to the lobby. I stopped at the main entrance and looked outside. Mom's bike leaned against a low brick wall in front of a planter. Barely in view, she crouched in front of Sam's wheelchair, touching her bandaged ankle. Her worried expression told me everything I needed to know. Getting away from her so we could go to Mosquito Lagoon might be impossible.

As I walked toward her, I refastened the flashlight to my belt. What could I say that would get her to let us go? The only thing that came to mind was the truth. I had to stop the next earthquake. No one else could. But telling her about Milligan's role in Dad's death could wait. That news should come from him.

When I walked over the collapsed portico's debris, she caught sight of me and ran with arms extended. I reached out as well. When we came together, she pulled me close. "Oh, Eddie, I'm glad you're all right. I was so worried about you."

I tried to pat her on the back, but my hand hit her backpack instead. "Yeah, I'm okay. Sam took some lumps, but she's tough."

Mom drew away and ran a hand through my hair. "What happened? Sam said she went flying off her bike and landed hard, but I couldn't get any details out of her. She said to ask you."

As people continued hustling past, their chatter made it hard to hear. I took Mom's hand and walked with her toward Sam and Barney. Sam sat in the wheelchair petting Prince Edward while Barney stood at attention, his rifle against his shoulder.

I sat on the brick wall next to the bike while Mom and Barney looked on. Now we were far enough away from the street to talk. I spread out my hands. "It's like this."

I told them everything — my nights out trying to fight crime, Damocles's death, my superhero invention, Sam's super powers, Damocles's hologram, facing kidnappers in the Dead Zone, meeting Mephisto and Graham on the roof of the Stellar building, and on and on.

Mom stared, her expression blank. Barney's face altered with every shift in the story, tensing during the dangerous parts, smiling at the funny parts, and even turning tearful when Damocles dissolved and disappeared.

I finished with, "So Sam and I have to go to Mosquito Lagoon and face Mephisto. I have to stop his plan to destroy Nirvana."

Mom gave me a long, hard look, her lips firm and her eyes unblinking. Then, her lips parted, and she inhaled as if ready to say something, but she shook her head and stared some more.

Finally, she stepped back and set a fist on her hip. "Well, Mr. Superhero, I'll tell you what. The city has to be saved. I'm going to let you and Sam go."

I blinked. "Really?"

"But there's one condition."

"What?"

She touched her chest. "I'm coming with you."

CHAPTER 17

Not My Kind of Water Slide

"But, Mom, it's dangerous. You might get hurt."

"*I* might get hurt? What about you?" She swept an arm toward Sam. "And your sister's already hurt. Would any mother in her right mind let you two go to that swamp alone?"

Her fiery eyes melted any objection I could come up with. "I guess you're right."

"Eddie." Mom set a hand on my knee in the same way Damocles had done. "You really are a superhero. There's no denying that. Damocles knows. I know. And Sam certainly knows. But every superhero needs to learn that he can't do everything by himself. That's why Damocles trained you to do what he couldn't."

I nodded. "Got any ideas on what I should do?"

Mom pivoted to Barney and altered to a commanding tone. "Do you have another gun?"

"An air pistol I use on rats. It shoots pellets. Won't kill humans, but it'll smart like the dickens."

"That'll have to do."

"I'll go to my office and get it. Anything else?"

"Eddie has his razor gun, so we're good on weapons." She unzipped my backpack, looked at the mattress, and rezipped it. "But we'll need a paddle. Anything that'll help us get across the swamp."

"I'll see what I can find."

When Barney left, I gave Mom another hug. Milligan's news about Dad weighed me down. I had to tell her. With Sam distracted by Prince Edward constantly begging for attention, now might be the best time.

Taking her by the hand, I walked a few steps away from Sam and whispered the confession, including my knowledge that Milligan is our half-uncle. She raised a hand to her mouth. A few tears slipped down her cheeks, but she managed to keep her composure.

She kissed me on the forehead and said, "Thank you, Eddie. Your father would be very proud of you. And I am, too."

When Barney returned, he carried a short paddle, a small handgun, an air pump, and a bundle of plastic. "Found my old rafting boat. Should be a lot better than an air mattress."

"Great. Thanks." I stuffed the deflated boat into Mom's backpack. Since she had only a couple of water bottles and three cereal bars inside, it fit without a problem.

Sam gave Prince Edward to Barney and set the air pump and paddle at her side, while Mom slid the gun into her pants pocket. We were ready to go.

After saying good-bye to Barney and the cat, we set out toward the city boundary, Mom on her bike and me pushing the wheelchair. When we merged into the crowded street, we slowed to a crawl.

I looked at the sky. The clock had ticked down to 9:41:19. We could make it to the address on Graham's card long before the quake, but would Mephisto be ready for us? The sooner we got there, the better.

As we drew nearer to the city limits, most people forked off onto wider roads, clearing the narrow street we had chosen. I looked to the rear. The pavement was deserted, except for a gray tabby cat trotting several yards back.

I groaned. "Prince Edward followed us."

Sam leaned to the side and clapped her hands in a calling gesture. "Prince Edward Thomas Oscar Stephen Horsey O'Ryan, come here."

We stopped and let Prince Edward catch up. He jumped into Sam's arms and settled into her lap.

Letting out a sigh, I looked back. Home lay at least two miles away. "What are we going to do with him?"

Mom stopped her bike and turned. She, too, gazed at the long stretch of road leading to our apartment. "Take him with us, I guess. With so many people leaving town, we'd be fighting against a stiff current if we tried to go home."

"Yay!" Sam held Prince Edward close. "I'll hold him in the boat. He won't be any trouble at all."

I mumbled in a sarcastic tone. "A cat in an inflatable boat riding over a swamp filled with snakes and scorpions. Sure. That won't be a problem."

We found a sign that said Mosquito Lagoon – Four Miles. An arrow pointed toward an even narrower street that led into a flat, grassy expanse. After we had traveled a few miles past the city limits, the sounds of the city faded.

Along the way, we drank from our water bottles, and Mom ate her cereal bars while Sam and I shared one of Victor's sandwiches — meatballs again. After we ate half of it, I wrapped the other half in its bag and stuffed it into my pocket for easy access, then put the second sandwich in my backpack.

Soon, a dirt road forked to the left, and a wooden marker identified it as Snakepit Gulley. We turned that way and continued on. Fortunately the dirt was hard packed, so the bike and wheelchair had no problem rolling over it.

The sun rose above a distant tree line. My legs ached. My head hurt. And we hadn't slept a wink all night. Yawns passed from me, to Sam, to Mom. Even Prince Edward yawned. But at least he could go to sleep in Sam's lap.

I checked my watch — 7:42 a.m. That meant eight hours and eighteen minutes till the big quake. Still plenty of time … I hoped.

The dirt road ended at a swamp. We halted and scanned the area. Cypress trees rose from the water, their split trunks resembling legs standing in floating green scum. A snake slithered over the surface, making a forked ripple in its wake — probably one of hundreds of serpents in this murky pool.

A thick spider web spanned a gap between two of the biggest trees. At the center of its intricate network, a huge black spider dangled, waiting for unsuspecting prey.

But scorpions? So far no sign of them.

At the far side of the swamp, a big house sat on a low hill. It looked like an ancient mansion, but from this distance, the details were fuzzy.

"Well," Mom said as she slid her backpack off, "no time like the present."

A mosquito stung the back of my hand. I slapped it, splattering blood across my skin. "No sign of guards. That worries me."

Mom slapped her neck, squashing another mosquito. "You mean, it's too easy? Suspicious?"

"Exactly."

"Good point, but we can't turn back now. We have to keep going."

I sighed. "You're right." Using the hand pump, I inflated the boat while Mom hid her bike in some nearby trees. Sam sat in the wheelchair and petted Prince Edward. Normally she would be bouncing around begging to help. Her ankles must have been hurting pretty badly.

When the boat reached its full size, I tossed the pump into it and looked it over. Obviously it was meant for one person, two at the most.

Mom flipped a switch on the air mattress. As its motor whirred, the material unfolded. Obviously its batteries still functioned. "You, Sam, and Prince Edward ride in the boat," she said. "I'll take the air mattress."

"But you're the heaviest of all of us." I picked up the paddle and handed it to Mom. "You and Sam and the cat ride in the boat. I'll take the mattress. Just make sure it's as full of air as it can get."

"I suppose that makes sense." Mom helped Sam

sit on the ground, then pushed the wheelchair into the trees next to the bike.

After Mom and Sam had boarded and shoved out a bit with the paddle, Sam reached for the cat. "Come here, Prince Edward Thomas Oscar Stephen Horsey O'Ryan."

I reached him toward her, but he twisted back and latched onto my shirt, digging his needlelike claws into my chest. As I pulled, I muttered, "If you don't go, you'll have to stay here and be snake bait."

"Don't you dare leave him here," Sam said. "He trusted us."

"You tell him. He's not buying what I'm selling."

After pulling and sweet talking the cat for another minute, I let him go. He still hung on, clinging to my shirt, though his claws no longer impaled my skin.

"Since he's so attached to you," Mom said, winking, "maybe you can get on the mattress with him."

"I'll give it a try." While Mom and Sam paddled farther out, I used my foot to push the mattress into ankle deep water, waded to it, and sat at the center. The cat hissed and again dug his claws into my skin.

"Ouch." I tried pulling him away, but that just made the pain worse. The mattress tilted from side to side, sending water over the edges.

Mom guided her boat next to mine, reached for my belt, and grabbed the spool's claw. As line reeled out, she said, "Just talk softly to Prince Edward, and we'll pull you along."

"All right." I looked up at the brightening sky.

No sign of any eagles. "Keep your eyes open for a trap."

Mom gave the spool claw to Sam. "Hold tight."

Sam clutched it. "Don't worry, Eddie. I've got you, and I won't let go."

"All quiet now," Mom whispered as she slid the paddle into the motionless water. "We don't want to startle the scorpions." With a silent stroke, she sent the boat forward. When she had paddled a few feet ahead, I locked the spool. The line tightened and pulled me along.

Another snake surfaced and swam parallel to the mattress. Its gray body and triangular head made it easy to identify — a cottonmouth. Fortunately, the cat didn't seem to notice. He released his claws and sat in my lap, though he stayed in an erect posture, his ears perked and eyes wide.

When Mom maneuvered around a cypress tree, another cottonmouth dropped from a limb and landed on the front of the mattress. I kicked it into the water. The cat hissed and leaped onto the material. His claws dug in and punctured it.

I jerked the cat up and tossed him over the water to Sam. She caught him and hugged him close. New hisses erupted, air leaking from the puncture points as the mattress slowly shrank.

Mom called, "Hang on" and dug the paddle into the water with furious strokes. We shot ahead. I clutched the edges of the mattress as it rode lower and lower in the water.

At a cypress tree to the left, scorpions rained from the branches and skittered along the thick scum toward my raft. With Mom's strong paddling, we surged ahead of them, but more scorpions converged from a tree to the right. As they crawled onto the mattress, I swatted them away, but they swarmed from all directions, too many to swat.

Three cottonmouths swam from one side and two from another, drawing closer and closer. "Mom! Hurry!"

"I'm trying!" She dug in hard and deep. What appeared to be a shoreline in the distance loomed closer and closer, but there was no way we could make it before the mattress and I would sink and be covered with scorpions and vipers. What could I do? I just kept beating the bugs with my hands and hoped I wouldn't get stung.

Ahead, we approached a gap between two giant cypress trees with a spider web stretched between them, draped high enough for us to pass underneath. An electronic eye was imbedded in each trunk, both pointing toward the gap. Could it be an alarm device?

"Mom, if we go between those trees, we might set off an alarm!"

"If I don't, you'll sink!" She paddled on, not slowing a bit.

A scorpion stung my wrist. Pain shot up my arm. I batted it into the water and bit my lip to keep from yelping. It felt like hot acid and an electrical jolt at the same time.

The boat shot between the electric eyes. A loud groan rode the air. Ahead, the swamp sank away, and we rushed into a downward plunge, taking water, snakes, and scorpions with us. Darkness enveloped everything. Although the venomous creatures disappeared in the murky depths, I kept swatting with both hands.

Seconds later, the angle eased. We rushed forward horizontally as if we were riding on a gentle waterslide. A door rose in front of us, opening to a lighted chamber. When we passed through, we dropped to a concrete floor and tumbled into each other, covered by tangled spool line, swamp scum, and scorpions.

CHAPTER 18

Spies? Would Spies Cross a Swamp On an Air Mattress?

Water surged over us and washed most of the scorpions away. As we righted ourselves, the door closed, shutting off the flow. Prince Edward shot out of Sam's arms and vanished in the room's dimness.

Sam spat out a wad of scum. "Yuck."

"Did anyone get stung or bitten?" Mom asked as she batted away what appeared to be the last of the scorpions.

"I got stung once." Now sitting with her and Sam on the raft, I showed her my wrist. Swelling and redness ran from my forearm down to my fingers.

She touched the wound. "Not much we can do about it. Let's hope it didn't inject a lot of venom."

As my eyes adjusted, our surroundings clarified. We sat in a cage with bars on three sides and a wall with a vertically sliding door on the fourth side. The cage appeared to be bolted to the wall and the concrete floor. The top — another set of bars — perched about four feet above the floor.

Opposite the wall, a closed padlock hung on the cage's hinged exit door. I sat on the wall side, Mom sat next to the exit, with Sam between us.

The cage stood in a spacious room with a nearby desk and high-back swivel chair. A computer and keyboard sat on the desk, apparently a workstation for whoever was supposed to guard our prison. A circular analog clock on a wall provided the time — 8:14 a.m. That meant less than eight hours remained before the big quake would strike.

I checked my watch. The digital readout agreed. The water hadn't damaged the mechanism.

A cottonmouth slithered under the desk and lay motionless in the shadow. No other snakes appeared anywhere, though scorpions sat here and there along the edges of the room

"Where did Prince Edward Thomas Oscar Stephen Horsey O'Ryan go?" Sam asked.

Mom pointed. "There."

I looked that way. The wet cat sat in a corner licking his fur. Sam called in a whisper, but he ignored her and continued licking.

Cramped and soaked to the skin, I untangled the tow line and drew it into the spool on my belt while Mom let the air out of the raft and gathered it and the deflated mattress into a corner of the cage.

I crawled to the cage's door and tested the latch and lock. They held firm. I then crawled to the door in the wall, but it wouldn't budge. Even if it opened, we couldn't possibly climb up the slide. "I guess with this automatic trap installed, they weren't worried about intruders. They'll just check the cage when they show up for work."

Sam climbed to her feet, short enough to stand, though her head brushed the top. As water dripped from her hair and clothes, she grabbed two bars over her head and shook them. The framework rattled but stayed intact. "How are we going to get out of here?"

Mom crossed her legs and looked around. "Do you see the padlock key anywhere?"

I scanned the desk, chair, walls, and floor. No key in sight. But with only a single fluorescent lamp in the ceiling, maybe shadows hid it from view.

The room's door opened, and more ceiling lights flashed on. "Well, well, well," a man called in a sarcastic tone. "What do we have here? Three rats caught in a cage?"

We all turned toward him. A lanky man in a security guard uniform stood with hands on hips, an amused expression on his face. "With this kind of catch," he continued as his gaze followed a scorpion skittering toward a wall, "I'd better call the exterminator. Both for the bugs and for the humans." He lifted and lowered his legs in turn, his shoes making ripples in the inch-deep water. "And I need to call the janitor."

"Where are we?" I asked.

"Don't pretend you don't know." He drew a handgun from a hip holster. "You weren't on a family holiday boat ride."

Sam shivered but stayed quiet. Mom gave the guard a hot glare. "Put that gun away. You're scaring my children."

"Shut it, lady." He pointed the gun straight at her face. "I know a spy when I see one. You're using these kids as cover."

"That's ridiculous. Do we really look like spies?"

The guard's eyes shifted as he scanned us. "Can't see what's in your backpacks. Hand them over. And the boy's belt, too." He pulled a key ring from his pants pocket.

While he searched for the right key, I stealthily unhooked my spool line and claw and sat on it. Although the claw pricked my skin, the pain might be worth it. With any luck, maybe he wouldn't see it.

The guard pinched a short silver key and opened the padlock, leaving the keys hanging in the lock. With his gun drawn, he lowered the cage's door like a drawbridge. "Push everything out."

Mom passed the paddle, deflated boat, and the wadded mattress to the guard. I unfastened my belt, shrugged down my backpack, and gave them to her. She handed them and her backpack over as well.

The guard shoved everything to the side and looked through the opening. "Now empty your pockets. Turn them inside out." We all obeyed. Sam produced a plastic frog, explaining that it was a copy of Princess Queenie's pet Horatio. The guard let her keep it. I withdrew the leftover sandwich, now soggy, while Mom reluctantly produced the pellet gun and extended it toward him.

The guard snatched the gun and smiled. "This and those gadgets on the kid's belt prove that you're really spies."

"Don't be an ignoramus," I said. "It's a pellet gun. To scare rats away."

"An ignoramus, huh?" He looked the gun over. "Okay, so it shoots pellets, but the belt has a knife and a gun."

I growled, "It's an air gun. It shoots little disks."

"But you had some other stuff. You spies can make escape gadgets out of bent paper clips and nose hairs."

"Even a soggy sandwich?" I asked as I passed it to Mom.

He took the sandwich, unwrapped it, and looked it over, smelling it twice. "I never seen a spy use a sandwich before." He tossed it back inside. When it landed next to me, it spilled open over its wrapper. Although the bread was falling apart, I repaired the sandwich and rewrapped it in case we got hungry later.

"Now I don't have to feed you." the guard said. "Not that you'll need any food if the boss decides to kill you." After closing the door and relocking it, he slung the keys onto the desk and set the pellet gun beside them. He pulled a phone from his pocket, punched in a number, and held it to his ear. "Yeah, boss. Got some news for you. We caught three varmints in the swamp trap."

"Twelve?" He squinted at us. "Well, the boy's kind of puny for twelve years old, but his face looks that age. Talks like he's thirty, though. The girl looks spot on for eight." He laughed. "Damocles? Mr. Graham, if Damocles was the third one, I don't think I'd be talking to you right now. He would've broken out of the cage, stuffed this phone down my throat, and strung me up by my toes. The third one's their mom."

I scowled. More proof Chet Graham really was in cahoots with Mephisto.

"Sure. No problem keeping them here that long. They ain't going anywhere. ... Right. See you then." He sat on the desk chair and began typing on the keyboard, his stare on the monitor. "Gotta put in a work order to get the janitor over here. He's not due till this evening, though. The trap's a great setup, but it sure makes a mess."

"How many others have you caught?" I asked.

"You're the first. Mr. Graham said it might happen soon. Said to watch for someone later today. If not for the trap, I guess you spies would've gotten through to Mephisto's secrets, but his genius inventions put a stop to that."

"What secrets?"

The guard laughed. "I know your tricks. I'm not giving anything away." He leaned back in his chair. "You might as well make yourselves comfortable. My boss won't get here for a while."

"He's right," Mom said as she settled into her corner. "We're all exhausted. Try to get some sleep."

I leaned closer and whispered, "Sleep? We have to figure out how to escape."

"Do you have an idea?" she whispered in return.

I shook my head. "Not yet."

"Then get some rest. Maybe we'll all think better when we're not so tired."

I slid to my corner, keeping the spool and claw under my thigh and the sandwich at my side. Sam snuggled up to Mom and closed her eyes.

For the next few minutes, I scanned the room, looking for something I could use to escape. What was out there? The cottonmouth lurked under the desk, but it was probably scared to show itself. Prince Edward lay asleep in a corner, out of the guard's sight. The keys sat next to the pellet gun, but the angle between them and me made them an almost impossible target for a spool line and claw. Not only that, throwing the claw would make a lot of noise. The guard would notice in a flash.

As my plans crumbled, my eyelids grew heavy. Maybe Mom was right. I needed to get some sleep. Just a couple of hours might be enough.

Although my wrist still hurt like crazy, sleep came quickly. Dreams flooded in. Swamps, scorpions, and snakes crawled over my body while Sam sat on a stump giving squirrels and butterflies ridiculously long names.

After what seemed like an hour of mental torture, my mind drifted into a dark void and escaped the madness.

CHAPTER 19

Meeting Mephisto ... Maybe?

Something wet and rough touched my hand. I snapped my eyes open. Prince Edward crawled into my lap, then quickly leaped off and gave me an indignant stare. My wet jeans must have repelled him. Since we hadn't fed him anything, he was probably hungry.

While I gave him a few long strokes, I shifted my gaze to the clock. It read 11:21 a.m.

The guard sat back in his chair, his eyes closed and his feet propped on the desk. A gentle snore emanated from his open mouth. Under the desk, the cottonmouth lay curled in darkness. This could be my chance. But everything had to work without a hitch.

Keeping my movements quiet, I unwrapped the sandwich and gave Prince Edward a sniff. He licked a meatball, but I jerked it away and laid the sandwich at my side.

While he stretched to get it, I took off his collar, pulled the spool from under my thigh, and attached the claw to the strap. When I refastened the collar to him, I left it on the loosest setting. After testing it to make sure it would slide off his head if I pulled hard enough, I reeled out several feet of line.

I gave Prince Edward another sniff of a meatball and tossed it onto the desk. It landed silently and rolled well past the keys. The cat ran between two bars and leaped up to the desk, taking the line with him. Padding softly, he trotted to the meatball and tore into it.

I tightened the line and pulled. The claw tugged on the collar, but Prince Edward stayed put, exactly as I had hoped. As I pulled harder, the collar slid over his head, pausing for a moment as he shook it off and continued eating.

The collar clinked on the desktop. The guard merely scratched his nose and slept on.

Pulling slowly, I dragged the claw and collar along the top of the desk, passing the pellet gun. When it drew close to the key ring, I pulled more slowly. The claw's hooks failed to catch the ring, but the collar slid over the keys and caught them in the center of the loop.

I clenched a fist. Yes. Now to reel my fish the rest of the way in.

Still drawing the line slowly, I glanced at the keys, then Prince Edward, then the sleeping guard, and then the coiled snake. So many things could go wrong. But I couldn't worry about maybes. I just had to keep pulling.

When the keys reached the edge of the desk, I stopped. Another inch and they would fall to the floor out of my reach. Catching them again with the collar might be impossible. I had only one option.

I gave the line a quick jerk. The keys flew to the floor two feet away and clattered loudly.

I reached out, grabbed the keys, and pulled the line in. After hiding everything behind my back, I leaned against the corner and closed my eyes to a narrow slit.

The guard shot to his feet and spotted Prince Edward on the desk. "Well, well, where did you come from?" As the cat finished the final bit of meatball, the guard picked him up and looked at our cage. He focused on me, but the only suspicious item in sight was the sandwich, now lying unwrapped next to my hip.

"Did you steal that boy's lunch? Shame on you." The guard touched the pellet gun on the desk and looked around the room, apparently not noticing the missing keys. He reseated himself with Prince Edward in his lap and stroked his fur. "Did you come in when they did? I thought spies always had black cats, not gray."

When he closed his eyes, I reached back and felt for the keys while scanning the room once more. The snake had uncoiled and now lay stretched out. Maybe it had been startled by the commotion. Still in the guard's lap, Prince Edward groomed himself, licking his paws and washing his face. Everything else remained as it was earlier.

I pulled the keys to my lap and crept toward the cage's door. Mom's head leaned against that side but not in the way. After finding the silver key, I reached over both her and Sam, slid my hand between two bars, and pushed the key into the lock. A quick turn snapped it open.

Mom gasped. I clamped a hand over her mouth and let out a quiet *shhh*. Her eyes wide, she nodded. I drew back my hand and grabbed a bar on the door. Together, we lowered it slowly and quietly until it rested on the floor.

After Mom crawled out, I climbed over Sam and joined her. While I put on my belt and backpack, Mom slid her arms through her own backpack straps, keeping every motion quiet.

When I finished, Prince Edward leaped and ran to me. The guard snorted and opened his eyes. I unfastened my razor pistol, dashed to the desk, and hunkered behind it. "Don't move." I aimed at him, grabbed the pellet gun, and threw it to Mom. She caught it and pointed it at the guard.

He raised his hands. "I knew it. You *are* spies."

I gestured with my head. "Let's get Sam out."

Mom lowered her gun and reached into the cage. While she helped Sam climb out, the guard eyed me closely, maybe planning to charge, possibly thinking I was a nervous kid who couldn't shoot. Not a bad guess. My gun hand throbbed, and my swollen finger barely fit through the trigger hole. I might not able to shoot him even if I tried.

I switched the razor pistol to my other hand. At that moment, the guard leaped and shoved the desk. It pinned me against the wall and slung my pistol away. He jerked out his own gun and aimed it at me. Gasping for breath, he barked at Mom. "Put your gun down or I'll shoot the boy."

"All right. Just take it easy." Mom bent over and set the pellet gun on the floor.

The guard refocused on me. "Now get back in the cage."

As Mom rose, she snatched the paddle and whacked the guard across the head, knocking his gun loose and sending him sprawling to the floor. A wild scream erupted. He leaped to his feet and ran to the door with the snake attached to his neck. Still screaming, he turned into a hall and disappeared from sight.

"Let's get out of here." I shoved the desk back, scooped up the three guns, and fastened the razor pistol to my belt while sliding the pellet gun into my backpack. I kept the guard's gun in my left hand, ready to shoot.

Sam picked up Prince Edward, and we hurried out the door, Mom supporting Sam as she limped. The guard had run to the left, so it made sense to head to the right.

We walked that way, slowed by Sam's gimpy pace. As we passed doors on each side, I checked every knob, but they were all locked. When we reached the hall's end and found no escape, we walked the opposite way, slower now as we passed the room with the cage and continued on.

At this end of the hall, we turned with the corridor to the right, then again to the left where we came to a long flight of stairs leading upward. Mom lifted Sam into her arms, and we trudged up the steps.

At the top, we walked into a huge lobby with windows all around, illuminating the room with sunlight. A tall door exited to the left, probably an entry / exit door for the building, and a hall led straight ahead into another wing.

I hurried to the door and opened it. About two hundred feet away, the guard jogged to the edge of the swamp where a boat sat tied to a tree. After untying the rope, he tripped and fell face first into the boat before righting himself and paddling away.

About halfway between the door and the swamp, a strange object protruded from the ground. It looked like an old-fashioned clothesline pole — a red metal rod sticking up and four silver rods at the top extending out at an upward angle. Four parallel wires spanned the gaps from one extension to the next all the way around. Maybe it was some kind of signal receiver that helped with guarding this place.

I turned toward Mom. "He's gone. We might be alone now."

She let Sam slide down and held her hand. "I wonder if he can find a hospital with all the turmoil going on."

"I'm not going to worry about him." I gave Mom the guard's gun and unfastened the razor pistol from my belt. "Let's search around. Maybe we can figure out where the earthquake machine is."

Again walking slowly, we ventured down the new hall. We tried door after door until one near the end opened. Extending the razor pistol while Mom readied her gun, I stepped inside with her and Sam and quietly closed the door behind us.

At the far end of the room, a grandfather clock stood near a window. Birds flitted about — canaries, parakeets, cockatiels, and crows. They flew between upright perches, hat stands, and wooden birdbaths filled with flowing water that spilled over the edges to surrounding drains.

A man dressed in a winged bird costume sat on a stool at the closer of two work tables. On the surface, a bright lamp shone on an open metal box as he tinkered with the innards using a tiny screwdriver. While he worked, he mumbled but paid no attention to us.

I edged closer and squinted. Unless other people in this hideout were required to wear bird costumes, this man had to be Mephisto.

Leaning toward Mom, I whispered, "Mephisto. I'm sure of it."

She whispered in return, "What are you going to do?"

"Force him to surrender." The razor pistol shaking in my grip, I called out, "Don't move, Mephisto."

He looked up from his work and stared at me, his brow bent low. "What a silly thing to demand. If I stopped moving, I would die. Heartbeats and respiration both require movement."

I blinked. He didn't act like Mephisto at all. "Don't try to con me, Mephisto. Just raise your hands and —"

"Why do you keep calling me that odd name?"

I tilted my head. "Aren't you Mephisto?"

"My name, young man, is Gilbert G. Godwin. Kindly address me as Gilbert, Mr. Godwin, or even triple G, but please refrain from using that moronic Mephisto moniker."

Sam piped up. "His voice is like Mephisto's."

He waved a hand. "Nonsense. I've never heard of the fellow. And if I had a name like that, I'd change it to Salvador or Stanley or even Sue. Mephisto is a wretched name."

I gestured toward the grandfather clock. "But we saw you in front of that clock with all the birds flying around. You called yourself Mephisto then. You and I talked about the earthquake, and you wanted to see my invention."

He scowled. "Poppycock, prattle, and … and … persimmon punch. If I am not here working, I am in my quarters reading, resting, or reciting rhymes. The only time I go near that clock is to wind it, and I certainly didn't talk to you. I have never seen you before in my life." He lowered his head and began tinkering again. "Now if you'll let me get back to work, I would appreciate it. Regulus brought me this interesting device, and I should like to explore it further."

"Regulus?" I refastened the razor pistol to my belt and looked on. My letter-A sticker adhered to the side of the box. "Is Regulus an eagle?"

"Yes." He kept his eyes on his work. "How did you know?"

"An eagle stole that device from me. It's mine."

"Yours?" He looked at me again. "You're rather young for a genius inventor."

Warmth rose into my ears. "Well, I am an inventor, but maybe genius is too —"

"Oh, don't stoop to self-deprecation just to satisfy expected norms. I know genius when I see it, and I will also be glad to keep you humble when I mention the flaws in your design."

"Flaws?"

"Yes, yes, of course. A few faulty flaws, and a fatal future."

"What do you mean?"

He turned back to my device. "Well, the theory behind it is ingenious. I assume that the emission excites expansion of molecular muscle mass in the target specimen."

"Yes, that's right."

He let out a tsking sound. "But the subject later loses strength and becomes ill, and the positive benefits of subsequent experiments are shorter lived with more extreme negative side effects."

"Right again."

He pointed at a dial setting behind my device's lens. "Too much gamma. Your mixture is potent, but it's too fast acting. The body is unable to adjust, and it rebounds in reverse. You need a slower increase. If you cut the gamma by twenty-three percent, the strengthening time will slow significantly, but the subject will lose strength more gradually with little to no negative side effects."

"Are you sure?"

He scowled. "Of course I'm sure, but my guess is that the mice you used were pre-pubescent females. Your device didn't work on males or older females. Am I right?"

"Um. I didn't use mice."

"Rats then. Hamsters. Gerbils. Small baboons. Whatever. Am I right?"

"Actually …" I gestured toward Sam. "My sister got zapped by it."

His voice erupted. "You experimented on a human? Your own sister? Why, that's a violation of scientific protocol of the highest magnitude. You should be ashamed of yourself. If there were a consortium of genius inventors, I would report your misconduct to —"

"It was an accident," Sam said. "I did it to myself." She lowered her head and her voice. "The first time."

"The first time?" Gilbert scanned Sam from top to bottom, pausing as he looked at her bandaged ankles. His voice calmed. "I understand now. The accidental experiment worked, but the young lady grew ill, and the only way you knew to help her was to try it again."

"Right," I said, nodding. "Exactly."

"How many times?"

"Three. She's recovering from the third one."

"And she is no longer ill, I assume."

"No more puking, if that's what you mean. Just sprained ankles from a fall. When she got recharged, they healed, but now they're sore again. I guess if I recharged her, they'd heal again, but I'm not sure."

"I see." Gilbert stroked his chin. "After she reached the lower parabolic extreme of illness, she recovered from nausea without any heroic intervention, though her muscular-skeletal structure is still weak."

I processed his rapid-fire words before answering with, "Exactly right."

"Why didn't you recharge her while she was ill the third time?"

"Because I thought —"

He waved a hand. "Never mind. It doesn't matter. The adjustment is the important issue. The only drawback will be a new uncertainty. Exposure will continue working on pre-pubescent girls. But on adults? Hard to say. I would experiment on animals to learn its new range."

"Good advice. I'll change the gamma."

"No need. I took it apart. I should apply my suggestion and put it back together."

While he worked, I stood in front of the grandfather clock, then pivoted and looked at the wall adjacent to the entry door. A projector-like box sat on a shelf with a lens pointing toward the clock. I found a switch on the box's side and flipped it on. Light emanated from the lens, but nothing appeared.

"That's a camera," Gilbert said. "It comes on by itself from time to time. I have no idea why. Never bothered to investigate."

I walked to a computer sitting on the farther table where a monitor and projector sat side by side. A stuffed crow with a metallic tag on its leg stood next to the computer. The monitor showed a crow in full flight, the same tag attached.

I turned on the projector. A few feet in front of its lens, a hologram of the crow appeared, flying in the same manner.

"Have you ever invented a hologram device?" I asked.

He looked at me, his brow lifting. "Yes, and a fine

invention it was. I have been able to photograph my birds and render them in full motion at any angle. It's especially helpful when studying an extinct species. Quite difficult to catch those in flight." He laughed. "I can even project a flying dodo bird. They never flew while they were on the planet, but they fly in my laboratory in all their dodo-rific glory."

I turned the projector off. "Did anyone ever take photographs of you from every angle?"

"My business associate did. He said he had an experiment of his own, but he never bothered to tell me about it."

"Is your associate named Chet Graham?"

"Indeed it is." He refocused on my invention. "Mr. Graham supplies me with whatever equipment I need for my work, a financier I suppose you might call him."

I turned to Mom. "I know what's going on."

"So do I." She slid the guard's gun behind her jeans waistband. "But I wouldn't have figured it out without your questions. You were brilliant."

I smiled. "Thanks."

"I have no clue," Sam said. "Tell me."

"It's like this. Chet Graham has a three-dimensional model of Gilbert, and he projects it as a computer-driven hologram whenever he wants to show Mephisto to people. When we were at the Dead Zone, Graham used this room as a background. With all the birds flying around, it looked real. I suppose he has Gilbert's voice print, too, so he can make his Mephisto model say anything he wants."

"What if Gilbert walks into the background while Graham is projecting?" Mom asked.

Gilbert adjusted the gamma dial, one eye closed. "If I am in this room, I am always at my workstation, unless I'm winding the clock, which takes only a few seconds, and I wind it only on Thursday afternoons at precisely five p.m."

Sam grinned. "So Mephisto isn't real. I knew it."

"Don't be smug." I tousled her hair. "Your head might explode."

Gilbert snorted. "Please, no exploding heads. My own head is ready to pop because that scoundrel has been using me for his nefarious purposes, and I don't want splattered brains littering my lab."

Mom rubbed my shoulder. "So what's the next step, superhero?"

"Stop the earthquake." I focused on Gilbert. "Did you ever invent a machine that causes earthquakes?"

He glared at me. "Heavens, no. Who in his right mind would want to do that?"

"Someone did. We had a few quakes in Nirvana, and Graham said someone stole his machine and used it to create the quakes."

"I did invent a machine that excites fault lines in a localized area in order to discover a way to minimize their damage. It was meant to detect shifts in advance so we could send warnings to those in danger. But such a tremor can hardly be called an earthquake. The experimental area is small, exactly the size of the field between this building and the neighboring swamp."

"Where is the experimental area?"

He nodded toward the front of the building. "The field between this building and the neighboring swamp. Remember, I said *exactly*."

"Oh. Right." I looked that way. "I saw a rod sticking up from the ground with four other rods attached. Is that the machine?"

"That is an antenna that allows for long-distance remote control. The device itself is underground."

"How does it work?"

"It sends a hypersonic signal to the underlying fault, which causes a minor shift, and the movement creates a tremor. But, as I indicated, since the fault is tiny and local, it cannot be felt outside of this immediate area. It is for research purposes only."

"Then how could the quakes in Nirvana happen? They were pretty big."

"A big quake can occur only if there is a significant fault under the city, but I'm not sure if Nirvana has such a fault."

"Can your device create a fault?"

Gilbert bent his brow. "Young man, are you suggesting the quakes are my fault?"

"No, I was wondering if your tremor device created a fault."

"If there is a fault under Nirvana, it certainly isn't my fault."

"Then whose fault is it?

"Isn't Nirvana your city?"

"Yes. I live there."

"Then it is your fault."

I pointed at myself. "I don't have a fault."

"No faults? Then you are a better man than I."

"No, I'm saying that Nirvana's fault isn't my fault. I didn't put it there. Someone else did."

Gilbert blinked. "Oh ... well ... why didn't you say so?"

I huffed a loud sigh. "I did say so. I just —"

Mom tapped my shoulder. "It's all right, Eddie. Let's figure out how Graham's using the device to make earthquakes."

I looked Gilbert in the eye. "Is it possible to use your invention to shift a fault under Nirvana and start an earthquake?"

Gilbert stroked his chin. "If the device's hypersonic signal could be transmitted close to the fault, then perhaps."

"What would it take to do that?"

"Oh, it would be tricky, I think, but it is possible. I duplicated the prototype, and the duplicate is portable, though because of its internal antenna, the remote must be within a mile of the device. Also, it would have to be embedded and anchored far under the city, which would require an excavation of mammoth proportions. The city officials would certainly be aware of such a project."

"Unless the person digging the huge hole had a magna-gopher."

"A magna-gopher?" Gilbert blinked. "Odd that you should use that terminology. I invented a digger for our project here that I called a robotic gopher — powerful, precise, and ..." He looked at me. "Can you think of a *p* word that works as an appropriate adjective? I enjoy alliterating in triplets."

"Portable?"

"Perfect. In any case, after we finished embedding the prototype transmitter here, I don't know what Graham did with the gopher. Do you?"

I nodded. "I think he parked it under the Stellar building in Nirvana and dug a deep hole to embed your duplicate hypersonic signaler."

"There is one certain way to find out." Gilbert rose from his stool and inserted his arms into his wings as if putting on sleeves.

"Why do you wear that bird suit?" Sam asked.

"To fly, of course." He walked to the window, opened it, and crouched on the sill. "You are welcome to follow me. I have spare sets of wings around here somewhere, but you might prefer going on foot." He leaped and, flapping his wings, disappeared from view.

I ran to the window. Gilbert flew about eight feet above the ground, his legs dangling awkwardly. As he made a wide turn, he appeared to be heading toward the front of the building where I had seen the antenna. After a few seconds, though, he crashed in a muddy bog and slid face first through the wet turf.

CHAPTER 20

Will the Real Mephisto Please Stand Up?

"He crashed." I looked at the ground — at least a six-foot jump down from the sill. Sam would never make it. "Mom, you and Sam head for the front door. I'll meet you outside. I gotta check on Gilbert."

Mom scooped Sam into her arms. "On our way."

I leaped out the window and landed with knees bent to absorb the impact. In a dead run, I crossed a wet field to Gilbert's crash site. He sat up, brushing mud from his face, his arms no longer inside his wings.

When I arrived, he spat out a glob of black mud and smiled. "A great success, if I do say so myself."

"Success? You flew like a dodo bird."

"Of course it was a success. It was my longest flight to date. It was terrific. It was tremendous. It was … "

"Triumphant?"

He grimaced. "No. Terrifying."

I grabbed Gilbert's arm and helped him to his feet. We walked around the building, slowed by his frequent stops — once to take off his shoes, dump out some mud, and put them back on; once to fold his wings and tuck them under his arm; and twice to brush more mud from his clothes.

When we arrived at the front of the building, I scanned the field for Mom and Sam, but they were nowhere in sight. "Gilbert, I'll be right back." I grabbed the razor pistol from my belt, jogged to the front door, and stepped inside, calling, "Mom? Sam?"

My voice echoed in the huge lobby. I looked out to the yard. Gilbert knelt at the antenna next to an open trapdoor about the size of a car's glove compartment, his hands out of view below the door, probably working with something underground.

I glanced at the hallways leading to the left and right, both vacant. Did Graham capture Mom and Sam? If so, since he needed me to contact Damocles, he probably wouldn't hurt them until he had me in his clutches. That meant I couldn't afford to look around and get caught in an ambush. Somehow I had to rescue them another way, but how?

I closed the door and jogged to Gilbert. "Is there a secret passage to get inside?"

He glanced past me, then answered in a whisper of his own. "Ah. Your familial companions should have come out by now, and you wish to rescue them, but I know of no secret entry." He looked toward the swamp. "I see tread marks. Mr. Graham must have arrived in the swamp crosser. It is an amphibious tank. It is quick, quiet, and …"

"Quake-proof?"

"Quagmire-proof. That's why it's perfect for driving through the swamp. He likely parked it in the back, saw your relations when he entered, and captured them."

"We could shake him up. That would give me a chance to get inside to help them." I nodded toward the antenna. "Is there any way we can generate a local quake? Enough to rattle the building?"

"Yes, the original hypersonic transmitter is still down there, which means that Mr. Graham is using the duplicate."

"Can you trigger the quake from here?

Gilbert shook his head. "Only the remote can trigger it. It would be foolish to trigger a quake while standing at the epicenter."

"Where is the remote? I could hide at your office window and start the quake from there."

"It's supposed to be here, so Mr. Graham must have taken it, proving that his intentions are disreputable, disgraceful, and despicable. But I have a spare in my office. It has fewer features, but it is functional."

"Will the spare remote work with the duplicate earthquake device?"

"No. The spare remote's frequency is locked on the prototype device here. The main remote can operate either the prototype device or the duplicate."

"So to get the spare remote, I need to find a way inside without anyone seeing me." I shook my head. "I'm back to the same problem. I need to come up with a different distraction." I eyed the tread marks leading from the edge of the swamp to around the building. "Is the swamp tank easy to drive?"

"Quite easy. The controls are standard, straightforward, and simple."

I imagined myself driving the tank, though I

wasn't sure what it looked like. "I'll guide it toward the swamp, jump out, and run to your office window. That should distract Graham long enough for me to get inside and find my mother and Sam."

"Finding them is one challenge. Actually rescuing them is another. Mr. Graham is not likely to simply hand them over. Since he usually travels with a muscular bodyguard who will likely be holding them, you will not be able to wrestle them away."

"Good point. Let's go ahead with the quake idea as a second distraction. I'll use the first one to get the remote."

Gilbert rubbed his hands together. "This should be a fascinating sequence of events. I will prepare the quake's direction and intensity from here. When you find the remote, just press the activate button and be ready for a sharp, shattering shake."

"Where in your office should I look?"

He shrugged. "I have no idea."

I let out an exasperated sigh. "It could take hours to find it."

"Not so." From his pants pocket, he withdrew a metallic wafer that looked like a small steel cookie. "I often lose remotes, so I invented this locater. Just push the button, and a light will blink faster and faster as you get closer to the remote. It works with the original controller or the spare."

"That'll help." I took the locator and slid it into my pocket. "What would you do if you lost the locator?"

"I would have to invent a locator locator and then perhaps a locator locator locator. As you can imagine, such a string of locators would soon become unmanageable."

"Okay. Let's get this started." I ran around the building toward the side I hadn't seen yet. When I got almost halfway, I came upon a machine that looked like a head-high miniature tank with a two-person seat on top. A hinged glass hatch stood open over the seat, ready to close on top of the passengers and keep them dry in the swamp.

Grabbing a handhold bracket on the side, I climbed up, hopped into the seat, and read the controls — a close-hatch button, a start / stop button, a forward / reverse / neutral switch, and a steering wheel. No problem.

After lowering the glass shield over my head, I pushed the start button. A quiet hum emanated from an engine below. Too quiet. I needed to do something to attract attention.

I flipped the switch to forward. The tank's big treads lurched and dug into the soft turf. As I steered it around the building and came into view of the front door, I tried to peek inside. No sign of movement anywhere.

Distraction time. I steered the tank toward the building's corner and rammed into it. The corner crunched as the metallic beast took out a huge chunk of wood. A gutter fell, and part of the roof sagged.

I shifted to reverse, backed away from the damage, and switched to forward again. As I rolled over the field between the swamp and the building, the front door flew open. A dark-haired muscular man dressed in military fatigues charged outside and sprinted toward me, shouting, "Stop!"

Judging by his speed and my distance to the swamp, he would catch me before I got there. No way did I want to get into a fight with this guy.

I opened the glass shield and jumped to the ground. The tank rumbled on. With a burst of speed, I ran toward the building, but the big thug dove at my legs, grabbed my ankles, and tackled me. I flopped to the muddy ground and tried to scramble away on all fours, but his vise-like hand stayed locked on my ankle.

As he rose to his feet, he lifted me high with one hand. I dangled upside down and swayed while facing him.

I shouted in a little kid's voice. "That tank thing is headed for the swamp. I left the hatch open, so it's gonna get flooded."

When he looked toward the swamp, his eyes flared. He dropped me and ran. I held out my hands, keeping my head from hitting the ground first, but the smack hurt my palms.

I scrambled to my feet and ran to the back of the building, wiping grass and mud from my face along the way. When I reached the window to Gilbert's office, I threw the claw into the opening, drew the line tight, and climbed in.

After auto-reeling the line, I withdrew the remote finder and looked over its features — an on-off button on one side and a tiny LED light on the other. When I pushed the button, the light blinked red about once each second.

I looked at Gilbert's worktable where my superhero device sat, now fully assembled. As I walked toward the table, the light blinked faster. I honed in on a drawer at one end of the table and opened it. Papers overflowed from inside, each one covered with scribbled drawings and mathematical equations. The light blinked like crazy.

While birds flitted here and there, I grabbed handfuls of paper and tossed them to the floor. A gray parrot landed on my shoulder and squawked about maddening, militant mosquitoes, but I tuned it out and continued hunting.

When I cleared the last piece of paper, a roundish black object no bigger than a key fob appeared at the bottom. I scooped it up and looked it over. A single red toggle switch displayed two labeled settings — on and off.

I slid it and the locator into my pocket, grabbed the razor pistol from my belt, and crept toward the office door. The moment I turned the knob, the door burst open. The muscular thug thundered in, making me backpedal. I shot at him, squeezing the trigger again and again. A razor disk sliced into his chest. Another grazed his chin. A third missed and stuck in a wall.

My next trigger pull resulted in a dull click. No more disks.

Roaring, the thug slapped the gun away. With a backswing, he hammered me across the cheek with his knuckles.

I stumbled and dropped to my bottom. Pain ripped through my skull. Spots blurred my vision.

But I couldn't pass out. Not now. I had to keep my head clear. Letting out a groan, I slid the knife sheath on my belt around to the back, hoping he wouldn't see it.

Behind the thug, Mom and Sam staggered into the room, pushed by Chet Graham at the point of a gun. Sam tripped over her own feet and tumbled to the floor next to me.

Whimpering, she grasped her ankle and whined, "Princess Queenie Unicorn Iris Ponyrider Buttercup Olive Lover Rosey Is Posey … is not happy."

Covering his bleeding chin, the thug jerked the razor from his chest and threw it out the window. He grabbed Mom's arm and shoved her to the floor with Sam and me. She fell to her bottom and pulled Sam close to her side. A nasty bruise painted Mom's forehead purple.

"They ambushed us," she whispered. "The smaller guy took my gun and bashed me in the head with it. I'm feeling really dizzy."

I leaned close. "That's Chet Graham. Just play it cool. I have a plan."

Graham aimed the gun at us and barked, "Where is Damocles?"

I glared at him. "How should I know? I'm just a kid. Why should he tell me where he is all the time?"

"Stop pretending, Eddie. I figured out that you're some kind of genius, and you invented a superhero generator that copies Damocles's powers. Now you and he are partners trying to create an army of superheroes. He wouldn't stray far without letting you know where to find him."

I sneered. "Shows how much you know. I have no idea where he is."

He gave me an I-don't-believe-a-word-you're-saying kind of smile. "All right. Then tell me why you're here instead of Damocles."

"I'm trying to stop the earthquake, of course."

"Mephisto told you how to stop it. He must be paid a billion dollars."

"Just cut the acting. I know you're behind the earthquakes. Mephisto doesn't even exist."

"Doesn't exist?" Graham laughed under his breath. "You have no idea what's going on behind the scenes. I'm just trying to be a go-between and deliver the ransom for the sake of our city."

I crossed my arms in front. For now, it might help to play along with his game. "Well, I don't have a billion dollars, and Damocles isn't here. What's your next move?"

He looked at the superhero device on the workstation. "I see you brought your invention."

I gave it a casual glance. "What about it?"

"If it works, I'll talk Mephisto into accepting it instead of the money. In the long run, being a superhero is worth more than a billion dollars. Even ten billion dollars."

"What makes you think it can make someone a superhero?"

"Mephisto saw through your pretense back in the Dead Zone. He figured out that your sister neutralized the muggers."

"What?" I set a hand on Sam's shoulder. "Look at her. Do you seriously think she could do that? And if my invention really could do what you say, all three of us would be superheroes, and you and your ugly partner would be nothing but a steaming pile of torn flesh and broken bones."

"I know what I saw. It just means your invention wears off after a while." He waved the gun. "Test it on me."

After glaring at him for a moment, I let out a sigh. "I guess I have no choice." I climbed to my feet and helped Mom and Sam get up. As I steadied Sam, I whispered, "Make sure the light hits you."

She gave no answer or nod. Either she didn't understand, or she knew exactly what to do and didn't let on.

I walked to the workstation and aimed my invention at Graham. "You'd better get a little closer."

He stepped over and stood directly in front of the lens. Mom and Sam waited off to the side, out of range. If Sam really knew what to do, she needed a countdown.

With my finger on the switch, I said, "I'll power it up on the count of three. One … two … three."

I flipped the switch. Sam crept over to Graham and crouched at his side. The ray washed over them, turning them both ghostly white. When the light blinked off, Sam sneaked back into Mom's arms.

Graham patted his torso. "I think it worked. I feel something."

I looked at Sam. If she felt anything, she wasn't showing it. Smart girl, as usual. Gilbert said the strengthening process would be slowed, so I had to be patient and wait for the perfect time to flip the earthquake switch.

As I reached into my pocket and grasped the remote, Graham extended a hand toward Lamar. "Shake."

When he complied, Graham's arm flexed. Lamar's face tightened more and more until he let out a groan and jerked away. "You nearly crushed my bones."

Graham smiled. "It seems to be working."

"Now are you going to tell Mephisto to stop the earthquake?" I asked.

"Perhaps, but I think he'll want to kill Damocles first. What good is it to have super powers if a superhero is out there who can stop him?"

"So you're planning to hold us here. Use us as bait to lure Damocles."

"Not me. Mephisto."

I poised my thumb on the earthquake button. It would be best to keep delaying until Sam showed some sign of super strength. I needed her help. "I'm not an idiot. You're Mephisto, and we all know it."

He laughed in the most unfunny way possible. "Very well. Now that I have what I want, I'll stop pretending. But you can't do anything about it. You can call me Mephisto, for all a name's worth."

I glared at him again. "All right, Mephisto. How are you going to let Damocles know we're here?"

"With a message in the sky, of course. It's worked quite well so far." Mephisto turned to Lamar. "Wait here. I'll get Dr. Godwin so we'll have them all in one place. Now that I have this invention, I won't need him anymore."

Lamar opened and closed his wounded hand. "But what if the little girl goes superhero on me? I saw her get zapped with you. Maybe I could beat her, but no use risking anything."

"Then we'll test our special handcuffs on her." He waved the gun toward the door. "You bring the cuffs and Dr. Godwin, and I'll make sure she doesn't cause trouble."

"Back in a minute." Lamar strode from the room and closed the door.

Mephisto flexed both biceps. "Yes, I'm getting stronger and stronger. Your invention will make me the richest man in the world."

I cast a stealthy glance at Sam's arms. They had grown slightly but not nearly as big as before. She could never take on Mephisto in a fight.

Less than a minute later, Lamar entered holding a set of handcuffs while pushing Gilbert in front. A black eye marred Gilbert's face, and his arm hung loosely at his side. Feathers clung to his sleeves, and his wings were nowhere in sight.

Mephisto nodded toward Sam. "Set the cuffs on medium shock and put them on her. When you close them, they'll activate in half a second, so let go immediately. Then she'll be in too much pain to be a superhero."

CHAPTER 21

Sometimes You Really Need an Earthquake

Lamar shoved Gilbert to my side and crouched in front of Sam. While he adjusted a tiny dial on the cuffs, my throat tightened. I couldn't let them shock my sister. But could I stop him by myself, even with an earthquake distraction?

Mom sidled up to me and stealthily withdrew my knife from its sheath on my belt. I could barely withhold a grin. She was ready to fight with me. Now to shake things up.

I flipped the earthquake switch. The ground shook hard. Everyone teetered and waved their arms to keep from falling. I leaped to Mephisto and snatched the gun away. Sam punched Lamar in the nose and sent him toppling backwards. His head crashed into a wall and cracked the plaster. Mom lunged and jabbed his forearm with the knife, making him drop the cuffs.

Trying to keep my arm steady in the rocking room, I aimed the gun at Mephisto as he braced himself against the door. "Don't move!" I shouted.

He raised his hands above his head. "I surrender. Just stop the quake."

I reached into my pocket and flipped the switch.

The room settled, though big cracks ran down every wall, and the door hung by only one hinge.

"So what now?" Mephisto asked, his hands still raised. "If you shoot me, you won't be able to stop the Nirvana earthquake. It's on a timer and will trigger on its own."

"I have an idea." I handed Mom the gun. "Watch him for me."

While she aimed the gun at him, I picked up the cuffs, turned the dial to maximum shock, and walked toward him with the cuffs extended.

Mephisto ripped the door from its hinge and threw it at Mom. She fired and hit his shoulder. The door slammed into her head and knocked her sideways, but Gilbert caught her with his good arm, keeping her from falling.

Bleeding from his shoulder, Mephisto staggered back, collided with the wall, and slid down to his bottom, stunned.

"Sam, help me cuff him!" I lunged and grabbed his wrist. He shook his arm to throw me off, but I held on like a pit bull. While I battled to put a cuff on his wrist, Sam clawed at his face, digging deep gouges.

I snapped one cuff closed and reached for his other arm. His free hand curled into a fist and punched me in the nose. I flew away and landed on my back.

Recoiling at the sudden move, Mephisto grimaced and reached for his wounded shoulder. Sam leaped at the chance and wrestled the other cuff onto his wrist, snapped it closed, and jumped to the side.

Electrical arcs raced across the cuffs. Mephisto closed his eyes in a tight grimace and moaned as he leaned his head against the wall. Still bleeding from the bullet wound and Sam's deep claw marks, he looked like he wouldn't give us any trouble.

Trying to catch my breath, I scanned the room. Mom sat on the floor, propped by Gilbert's hand on her back. Awake but woozy, she smiled and whispered, "Good job, son."

"Indeed," Gilbert said. "You and your sister are amazing. You're astounding. You're ..."

"Astonishing?" Sam offered.

He nodded. "Affirmative."

Lamar let out a moan, though his eyes remained closed. Our time was running out.

I spoke to Mephisto with a commanding tone. "Tell me how to stop the earthquake."

Gritting his teeth, he spat his words in pain-filled spurts. "Get lost. ... These cuffs ... will run out ... of power eventually. ... Then I'll kill you all."

I eyed the cuffs. Setting them at maximum was necessary, but no battery could keep that kind of charge going for long. "We'd better get out of here."

"But how do we cross the swamp?" Mom asked.

"Mephisto has a swamp tank. Two people can ride in that, but two others will have to find another way."

Gilbert raised a finger. "As I mentioned earlier, I have spare sets of wings. Two of us can fly while the other two ride in the tank."

I nodded. "Get them, and let's go."

While the electrified cuffs continued shocking

Mephisto, Sam pulled Mom to her feet, and Gilbert collected two sets of wings from a closet. I carried one, Sam carried the other, and Mom hauled my superhero device in her backpack.

After tying Lamar's wrists with a computer power cord, we walked out as fast as we could, hoping for the best.

When we reached the front door, Sam tugged on Gilbert's sleeve. "Have you seen a cat around here?"

He shook his head. "Neither hide nor hair nor haunches of any feline."

Sam cupped her hands around her mouth and called, "Prince Edward Thomas Oscar Stephen Horsey O'Ryan. Come here, kitty."

I grasped Sam's wrist. "We don't have time. He's probably —"

"There he is." The gray tabby scampered across the room and leaped into Sam's arms.

With the cat in tow, we hurried on. When we arrived at the swamp, we found the tank sitting at the edge with the hatch open.

"So who flies and who rides?" I asked as I gave the remote locator back to Gilbert.

Gilbert slid the locator into his pocket. "You and Sam should fly, of course."

"Maybe you'd better fly with her. She's strong enough, but I've never done it before. I can drive the swamp tank."

Gilbert rubbed his shoulder. "When that Lamar fellow ripped my wings from my arm, he wrenched my shoulder. I can barely move it at all. And surely your mother is in no shape to fly."

"I suppose you're right." I narrowed my eyes at the swamp. "You said the distance you just flew was your record. How far did you fly?"

"Oh, I suppose about two hundred feet."

"And how far is it to the other side?"

"Perhaps six hundred."

"*Six* hundred? That's triple your record."

"True, but you are vigorous. You're vivacious. You're vital. And Sam is ... well ... she's Super Sam."

"Maybe we can ride on top of the tank."

Gilbert shook his head. "The swamp's too deep. You would submerge and have to swim through snakes, scorpions, and spiders. All quite venomous."

I gave him a resigned nod. "So I'll fly ... I hope."

After Gilbert gave us quick verbal lessons on how to operate the wings, I stared at the swamp's maze of cypress trees. Spider webs spanned the gaps between nearly all of them, each with a huge hairy spider lurking in the strands. "It'll be like a fly trying to get past an army of hungry frogs."

"True, my young friend. Just try to stay ahead of us. If we see you fall in, we'll stop and try to help somehow, that is, if the snakes, scorpions, and spiders don't get you first."

I cringed. "Thanks a lot."

Gilbert pointed toward the swamp. "Be sure to stay above the electric eyes when you fly past those two central trees. Otherwise, a door at the bottom will spring open, and our underwater crossing will end in a hurry."

I scanned the swamp to the left and right of the booby-trapped trees. Other trees grew tall and dense all around. Flying between the two central trees was our only option, though a thick spider web ran across the gap. "We'll make it somehow."

After Sam passed Prince Edward to Mom, she and Gilbert climbed into the tank and closed the hatch. Sam leaped on top and launched into the air. Flapping her wings, she flew in a clumsy up-and-down path over the swamp, but with powerful arms and a light body, she stayed aloft without a problem.

I clambered up and beat my wings as hard as I could. At first, nothing happened, but after a few seconds, my feet lifted off. I angled my body and flew above the swamp, but every time I raised my arms to flap, I plunged. Then when I dropped close to the scummy water, I thrust my wings downward and rose again just in time.

With each repetition, I dropped closer to the swamp. At this rate, I would face plant in the snake-and-scorpion-and-spider-infested soup long before I could reach the other side.

I looked back. The swamp tank rolled into the water and disappeared below the surface, hidden by the murky liquid, though bubbles on the surface gave away its presence.

Ahead, Sam circled back toward me, calling out, "Need help, Eddie?"

"Not yet." I again dipped low, this time skimming the water with my shoes before rising once more. Straining to get higher, I grunted, "But stay close, just in case."

We flew side by side, dipping and rising. As we drew nearer to the two trees, I timed my rises and falls. I had to dive right before I reached the electronic eyes, lift over the invisible laser shooting from one to the other, and knife through a narrow gap between the bottom of the spider web and the laser line. Getting through the gap with flapping wings would be tricky. Or maybe impossible.

Shots rang out to the rear. A bullet whizzed past my left wing. Another plunked into the water below. I shouted, "Faster!"

A bullet slammed into the tree on the right. Scorpions swarmed down the trunk and crawled onto the water, staying afloat on the scum. A snake dropped from a limb and swam across the swamp just below our path.

As more shots fired and bullets zinged past, I dropped low with the wings' upstroke, then whipped them down to get over the laser, but my legs hit the water. As I rose, something crawled up my ankle and stung it.

Pain surged. My wings sagged. I dropped for a split second before flapping again, but I passed directly between the electronic eyes, though I missed the web. Sam crashed right into the sticky strands and flew on, silk plastered across her face.

Below, the water sank. A flushing sound gurgled. As I continued rising, I looked back. In the draining swamp, the tank appeared, stuck in the open trapdoor. Since it couldn't close because of the huge machine, water, scorpions, and snakes streamed into the hole.

At the swamp's edge, Graham and Lamar each aimed a gun our way. Fortunately, our erratic flights made them miss, but the water was receding quickly. Soon they would be able to move closer and get a better shot.

The tank gunned its engine and rocked back and forth, but it couldn't lift from the hole.

"Sam," I shouted, nearly exhausted. "Can you help Mom and Gilbert?"

Her face covered with spider silk, she reversed course. "But my arms are in my wings."

"Just use your head. You'll think of something."

"I'll try." With bullets still zipping past, she flew into the hole. Seconds later, the tank surged out and drove onward. Sam appeared behind it, pushing with her head while flapping.

I landed on the top of the tank and shed my wings. While standing on them, I reached down, grabbed Sam's shoulders, and hauled her up. When I settled her on top of the tank, I ripped some of the webbing from her face. "Now *that's* using your head."

Another bullet zinged by. We crouched low. Graham and Lamar trudged into the drained swamp, shooting less frequently as they labored through the muck.

Graham surged ahead, his supercharged legs pushing through the quagmire, but when he drew near the closed trapdoor, he stopped. His eyes shot wide open. Between us and him, five snakes slithered his way.

As he backed up, he shook a fist and shouted, "Go ahead, fools. You can't stop the earthquake without me. When you fail, tell Damocles to meet me at the remains of the Stellar, and bring the superhero generator. Or else." He turned and hurried to the swamp's edge, Lamar at his side.

Sam made a razzing noise with her lips. "He's a turnip head."

"A turnip head?" I sat and pulled up my pant leg. Although the scorpion was gone, a swollen welt on my ankle hurt like crazy. "What's a turnip head?"

Sam withdrew an arm from a wing and pulled more web strands away from her face. "They're bad guys on the Princess Queenie show. The henchmen for Onion Man."

I smirked. "So I guess they're garden-variety villains. We shouldn't root for them."

"What? I don't get it."

"Never mind." I turned and focused ahead. The swamp's edge drew near. Soon, the tank rolled out of the muck and up to dry land, close to where we had left Mom's bike and Sam's wheelchair.

I scanned the sky toward Nirvana. The hologram timer had vanished, replaced by a message of some kind, too far away to read. I checked my watch — 2:04 p.m. Just under two hours till the quake. We had to hurry.

Leaving the bike, wheelchair, and wings behind, we rolled on. When we drew close to the city limits, hundreds of people streamed in from the highways on foot, on bikes, and in carts. But why?

I looked at the sky. Now the message was readable — Earthquake Stopped by Damocles. Return to Your Homes. All is Well.

I gulped. Mephisto did that to lure people back

to the city. He wanted to kill as many as possible and pin the blame on Damocles. He knew I would tell Damocles to come to the Stellar building with my invention. He planned to kill Damocles there and become an omnipotent supervillain.

And I had to stop him. Of course, Damocles was already dead, but I had to keep him alive in the hearts of the people of Nirvana. No one else could do it.

Again we weaved through the crowds and wrecked vehicles, but this time the people weren't so rushed and pushy. Lots of eyes turned our way, and no wonder. It's not every day you see two kids riding through town on a miniature tank.

I thought about warning people to reverse course, but who would believe our crazy story? I couldn't contradict the message in the sky without better evidence that it wasn't true.

Gilbert operated the tank like an assault vehicle, shoving cars out of the way and even driving overtop a few. We stopped at our apartment to use the bathroom and grab a bottle of water for each of us before hurrying on.

When we passed by Magruder's and the triage unit, I peered into the tent area. Milligan sat on an examination table while Dr. Ross pulled a needle and thread, stitching a cut on his cheek.

Milligan's eyes widened. He tried to get up, but the doctor pushed him back down, saying something inaudible.

We continued into the downtown area until we stopped near the edge of the gorge where I found

Sam earlier. The lengthy journey helped a lot. The swelling from the scorpion sting lessened, though it still hurt, and Sam had time to strip off the rest of the spider silk.

I looked again at my watch — 3:17 p.m. Only forty-three minutes to go.

After we climbed down, Mom got out of the tank and joined us at ground level, still wearing the backpack that carried my superhero generator. Holding Prince Edward, Gilbert stood atop the tank and looked around while rotating in place. "The city has been devastated, demolished, and …"

"Destroyed?" I offered.

"Definitely."

I attached my spool's claw to an iron bar embedded in broken pavement and reeled out some line. When I was ready, I looked at Mom. "I don't think you and Gilbert can come with us."

She nodded, tears sparkling in her sad silvery eyes. "I'm okay with that. You and Sam are the superheroes." She kissed my forehead, then Sam's. "I know you can do this."

Warmth spread across my skin. That was the best compliment I could ever ask for. "Thanks, Mom."

"Should we just stand here and wait for you to come back?"

I looked toward the Stellar building, now just a ragged shell about a quarter as tall as before. "See if you can drive the tank to the Stellar and find Graham. Maybe hide close by and see what he's up to. When we stop the quake, we'll come back and find you."

Mom crossed her arms, fidgeting. "Okay. We'll be waiting."

"Unhook the claw when we get to the bottom. All right? This one doesn't have an automatic release."

"Will do."

I looked down into the gorge. Water no longer fell into the depths. Someone had probably shut off the hydrant's feeder valve. In any case, Sam couldn't jump that far without risking another injury, and she didn't know how to rappel.

I took off my backpack, handed it to her, and crouched. "Ready to ride down?"

"Yeppers." She climbed onto my back and raised a fist. "Let's put the brakes on the quake."

CHAPTER 22

When Carrying a Superhero on Your Back, Don't Tell Her that She's Heavy

With Sam on my back, I let out spool line and descended into the gorge. Her weight pulled against my shoulders, making them ache. Sweat moistened my shirt. Each time I pushed against the rock with my legs, I grunted.

"Are you all right?" she asked.

"Just tired. Not enough sleep. And you're not exactly a feather."

"Sorry. I'm super strong now. I could've jumped down like I jumped up before."

"Last time you nearly broke your ankles. But it's all right. We're almost there."

When we reached bottom, she leaped down and bounced on her toes. "I still feel good."

"Has your strength worn off at all?"

"Maybe a little."

I nodded. "Gilbert said it would be gradual. Let's hope it lasts." When Mom released the claw, I reeled the line into the spool while Sam helped me put my backpack on.

Although the sun shone into the gorge, daylight wouldn't be able to follow us underground. I unhooked the flashlight and aimed the beam into the tunnel as we walked in. I trained my ears for any noise ahead, but all was quiet, no sound from the generator.

Half walking and half skipping at my side, Sam looked up at me. "How do we know that old Turnip Head won't be there waiting for us?"

"Because he doesn't know that we know where the transmitter is."

"But what if we don't know that he knows that we know where the transmitter is?"

"How could he know that?"

"Because he knows that we know we wouldn't be going back to Nirvana unless we know where it is."

"But he doesn't know that we know that Damocles is dead. He thinks he knows that we know Damocles is the only person who can stop the earthquake, so he thinks that we think we're going to Nirvana to find him."

"You think so?"

"I know so."

"I hope so."

After a few minutes, the beam landed on the sofa, now sitting in darkness. A quick sweep of light from wall to wall revealed no one in the chamber.

We walked together to the hole and peered into it. The depths seemed to swallow the light, giving no hint about the mysteries that lay below.

I found a pebble and dropped it into the hole while looking at my watch. When it struck bottom and the click reached my ears, I calculated the distance, taking into account the time it took for the sound to return. "It's about eighty feet down."

"How long is your line?"

I touched the spool on my belt. "This one belonged to Damocles, so I'm not sure. My spools are a hundred, so his are probably at least that long. We should be fine." I reeled out the spool's claw and searched for a place to attach it. "Ready to ride on my back again?"

She shook her head. "It's too far down. You'll get tired. I should climb on my own."

"I know you're strong enough, but it takes practice. I've done it a hundred times."

"And I watched you lots of times. Let me try. You go first, then I'll pull up the line and go next."

"But you don't have a belt."

"Then send the belt up, too."

"And leave you alone up here? Uh-uh. Not a chance. And I can't let you go first, because then you'd be down there by yourself. That would be even worse."

Sam crossed her arms in her I've-made-up-my-mind-to-be-as-stubborn-as-a-concrete-mule pose. "I'm not gonna ride on your back again. You're already too tired."

"All right. No time to argue. You wear the belt and go first. With the spool attached, it's safer than riding on my back anyway. It has an automatic brake if the line spins out too fast. I'll rappel right above you so you won't be alone."

I attached the claw to the generator, but when I tested my weight against it, it dragged. Sam and I heaved it onto the sofa, then I attached the claw to the sofa's leg. The combined weight proved to be enough of an anchor.

After fastening the belt to Sam's waist and showing her how to use the spool mechanism, I gave her the flashlight and whispered, "Let's stay quiet until I say otherwise."

While I put my gloves on, she set her feet against the hole's edge, leaned over the opening, and lowered herself, letting line out as she walked backwards down the hole's wall.

I copied her actions, my hands holding the line above her. Below, a dim red glow appeared and disappeared, as if blinking.

When Sam reached bottom, she whispered, "That was easy."

"Shhh." Following Sam's waving flashlight beam, I touched down. After readjusting my backpack straps, I took the flashlight and scanned the area — an enormous dugout chamber. A few steps away, a cubic box about the size of a basketball sat on the rocky floor. On top, a line of digits flashed red, changing every second — 00:16:14, 00:16:13, 00:16:12.

Beyond the box, a tunnel ran out of sight in an upward slope, probably the way the magna-gopher exited this place, but where on the surface did it come out? Maybe Mom and Gilbert would see it up there.

Sam whispered, "Is that the quake thingy?"

"I think so."

"Maybe we can just carry it out of here."

"Let's see how heavy it is." I crouched, slid my

hands under the box, and lifted, using my legs to help. The unit stayed put. As Gilbert had said, it was anchored, maybe by concrete slabs buried underneath it.

"Let me try." Sam went through the same motions to no avail.

I dug the spare remote out of my pocket and flipped the switch both ways. The timer marched on, now well under sixteen minutes. "Maybe you can tear it apart with your super —"

Something squealed, like spool line shooting out at hyper speed.

Sam screamed, "Eddie!"

She lifted off the floor. I dropped the flashlight and remote, leaped, and threw my arms around her waist. As we rose together, I felt for the spool on the belt. By the time I found it, we had risen too high. If I detached it now, we would fall to our deaths.

Sam growled. "It must be Turnip Head."

"Just stay calm. We'll figure something out."

Above, light appeared at the top of the hole, and the sound of an engine drifted down. Mephisto must have restarted the generator and turned on the lamp.

When we rose into the upper room, Mephisto slung the line down, throwing us to the floor. "Now you will be the ones to suffer." His face gouged and bloodied, he displayed a pair of handcuffs and lunged toward Sam.

I jumped up and plowed into him with both fists, aiming at his injured shoulder, but his backhanded slap sent me flying to a wall. I slammed into it butt first, bounced, and rolled up to hands and knees.

Every limb trembling, I crawled toward Sam. My spine tingled. My head pounded. The entire world spun. I would never get there in time to help.

As he put the cuffs on her, she fought like a wild horse, bucking and flailing. Both she and Mephisto seemed to be tiring. The superpower charge was wearing off.

Finally, Mephisto pushed Sam against a wall a few steps from me, snapped the cuffs on her wrists, and stepped away. Electricity shot across the chain between the cuffs. She arched her back against the wall, wincing and whimpering.

With each wince, I winced with her. Her pain tore into my gut. I had to stop the torture. But how?

Mephisto turned toward me. Sweat glistened on his forehead in the glow of the floor-standing lamp. He spoke through halting gasps. "Now perhaps you … will be persuaded to give me the superhero device. Once I have it … I will stop the transmitter's countdown, but I will take the remote with me. If you try to follow … I will restart the clock."

He took a deep breath, settling his voice. "The time it takes you to release your sister will be enough for me to get away."

I struggled to my feet on shaky legs and glanced at my watch — 3:49 p.m. Only eleven minutes to go.

"To further incentivize you," Mephisto continued, "Lamar dug a hole with my magna-gopher, and your mother and Gilbert are at the bottom. If anything goes wrong here, Lamar will bury them alive. I'm in touch with him by radio, so I can order their executions in two seconds."

I concealed a swallow. Lamar was a moron. He probably didn't look inside Mom's backpack for the superhero device.

I crossed my arms and clenched my gloved hands, taking on what I hoped was a brave-looking pose. "Your superpowers are almost gone."

"I know, but I'm more than a match for you even without superpowers." He unclipped a radio from his belt and raised it to his lips. "Now shall I order your mother's execution, or will you tell me where your invention is?"

Sam moaned, her eyes tightly shut and her teeth gnashing. I couldn't let this continue for another second. "Let Sam go, and I'll tell you. Or put me in the cuffs instead. Just stop torturing an innocent little girl."

"Attempts to shame me won't save your mother." He walked close to me and produced a tiny key from a pocket. "All right. You can take Sam's place, and you'll stay in the cuffs until you give me what I want."

I snatched the key and lunged to Sam. With quick moves, I unlocked the cuffs and threw them at Mephisto, my gloves keeping the shocking jolts at a minimum.

As we sat together, Sam slid her arms around my neck and sobbed. "Oh, Eddie. Thank you. You're a real superhero."

"Your turn to wear them," Mephisto said as he bent over and picked up the cuffs.

Sam unzipped my backpack, her sobs masking the sound.

"What are you doing?" Mephisto grabbed Sam's arm and shoved her to the side. "What are you hiding in that backpack?"

I sighed. Mastix was still in there. No use trying to hide it. It wouldn't work for him. "See for yourself." Still sitting close to Sam, I shrugged the pack down, slid the straps from my arms, and extended a strap toward him.

He snatched the pack away and looked inside. "A sandwich?"

Sam hugged her knees against her legs and pouted. "Being a superhero made me hungry. I was trying to get it."

The urge to feel behind my back nearly overwhelmed me. Had Sam hidden Mastix there?

Mephisto pulled the smashed sandwich out and threw it at Sam. "Stupid kid."

While he was distracted, I lifted my bottom and slid back. Mastix now lay between my legs. But would it work? I closed the gap to hide it and looked at my watch. Five minutes to go.

Mephisto stooped and slapped the cuffs on my wrists. When they snapped in place, he took the key and my gloves and stuffed them into his pocket as he stepped back.

The cuffs lit up. Shocks rocketed up my arms, into my brain, and down my spine. Pain — horrible, torturing pain — ripped through my body from head to toe. My limbs stiffened. I couldn't move my legs or arms to reach for Mastix.

Mephisto roared at Sam, "Where is the superhero generator?"

She glanced at me with tear-filled eyes. I couldn't tell her what to do. I could barely breathe.

Firming her lips, she got up, set her fists on her hips, and glared at Mephisto. "My mother has it, Turnip Head."

"Little twerp." He backhanded her across the cheek. She toppled to her side and braced herself with a hand on the floor.

I choked out, "Coward."

"The slap was for the lie. I want the truth."

Grimacing, Sam held a hand over her cheek. "I'm telling the truth. Our mother has it."

"We'll see about that." Mephisto raised the radio, pressed a button, and spoke into it. "Lamar, the kids say their Mom has the superhero invention. Have you seen it?"

While he listened to the answer, I forced my stiff legs apart, revealing Mastix. I lowered my trembling arms toward it. Even if I could grab it, would it work? Would it finally recognize me as a superhero? It was our only hope, but the shocks were rattling my brain. At any second, they might knock me out.

"What do you mean they escaped?" Mephisto yelled. "How could they escape?"

I whispered to Sam, "Help me."

As she edged toward me, Mephisto barked into the radio. "Catch them and kill them. Then get the device and start the chopper. I'll meet you there." He refastened the radio to his belt and looked at me.

Sam halted, her arms stiff at her sides.

"Your invention is obviously not here," Mephisto

said. "If your mother really has it, it will be mine in mere moments."

"What are you going to do with us?" Sam asked.

"Since you're still strong, it might take a while to kill you. I'll just leave you here to die, buried by the earthquake."

CHAPTER 23

Are Wishing Wells for Real?

Sam leaped to me, grabbed Mastix, and put it in my hands. The thongs brightened. I whipped them toward Mephisto. Each thong shot out a shimmering bolt. The bolts surrounded him with an electric web that trapped him in place. He spread his arms and stiffened, a terrified expression stretching his bloody, gouged face into a hideous mask.

Still jolted by the cuffs, I hissed, "Get the key."

"But he put it in his pants pocket," Sam said. "I can't get through all that electricity, can I?"

I lowered Mastix and willed the bolts to stop. When they died away, Mephisto collapsed.

Sam jumped to him, fished the key from his pocket, and hurried back to me. She unlocked the cuffs and helped me get them off.

Sizzles invaded my ears. My eyes burned. But I couldn't let the fiery pain stop me. I transferred the gadgets belt from Sam's waist to mine, then fastened Mastix to it. The line we used earlier was still attached to the belt spool. No need to reel it in.

I tried to look at my watch, but a fuzzy glaze coated everything. "Does it say three-fifty-seven?"

Sam squinted at it. "Yep."

"Three minutes to go." I set the readout to show the minutes and seconds till four p.m. The blurry digits showed 2:51 … 2:50 … 2:49. "Let's get down to the transmitter. Maybe I can destroy it with Mastix."

Sam helped me to my feet. "What about Mom and Gilbert? Lamar's going to try to kill them."

"We'll see about that." I ripped the radio from Mephisto's belt. "See if you can find the remote."

While Sam dug through his pockets, I held the radio to my lips, pressed the talk button, and spoke with a low, gravelly voice. "Lamar, did you kill those two yet?"

"Boss, are you all right? You sound strange."

"No time for explanations, you fool. Just answer the question."

"I got 'em trapped. I was just about to bury them with the gopher."

My throat narrowed. I couldn't keep my voice low. "Leave them and pick me up in the chopper. We have less than three minutes left."

"Hey, you're not Graham. Who is this?"

"Your worst nightmare." I tossed the radio to the sofa. Did I help Mom and Gilbert at all? Or did I make things worse?

Sam pulled a small black object from Mephisto's pants pocket. "Got it."

"Let me see." When she handed it over, I scanned a row of tiny red buttons — a start/stop switch, a frequency modulator, a timer-change dial, and a lock/unlock toggle. I tried to flip the first switch to stop, but it wouldn't budge. The timer dial wouldn't move either.

I set my thumb on the locking switch. A red light came on underneath, and a voice emanated. "Print not recognized."

"It's protected," I said as I stumbled to Mephisto, the spool line dragging behind me. When I reached for his hand to get his thumb, he slid it away and rose to all fours. I backpedaled a few steps and tossed the remote into the hole. Now he couldn't use it against us.

Mephisto glared at me, his focus on Mastix. Saying nothing, he climbed to his feet and staggered into the tunnel in a daze.

An urge to follow and check on Mom stormed in, but I had to stop the quake or everyone would die.

I limped toward the hole. "Sam, find the claw and hook it to the sofa again."

While she complied, I detached the penlight from my belt, grabbed the line, and crouched next to the hole's edge. When she finished, I gave the line a tug. "It's secure. Now get on my back."

She climbed on. "Ready."

I handed her the penlight. "Keep me updated on what my watch says."

"Roger dodger."

I rappelled down. While I descended, Sam set the penlight's thin beam on my watch and called out the remaining time. "Twenty-five seconds … twenty … fifteen."

I dropped faster. Since I forgot to retrieve the gloves, the line burned my hands. But no matter. The pain was nothing compared to getting crushed by the entire city of Nirvana.

When we reached bottom, Sam jumped off my back. "It's under four."

I pointed. "Shine the light on the transmitter."

The beam shifted to the box. Its timer showed two seconds. I grabbed Mastix from my belt and whipped the thongs. The sparks shot out and created an electric web around the transmitter, but the skinny bolts did no damage.

The clock ticked to zero. The transmitter emitted an ear-splitting squeal. The ground shook. Rocks fell all around, some striking our heads and shoulders, though they seemed to have no effect on the box.

I whipped the thongs again, this time with the special wrist action Damocles taught. A brilliant bolt shot out and slammed into the transmitter, now half-buried in debris. It exploded, sending rocks and shards flying toward us.

I jerked Sam down and crouched over her. As sharp objects slashed my back, I bit my lip hard. Pain knifed into my body. Warm liquid trickled down my skin. Rocks and dirt rained, pelting my head. The squeal had silenced, but the shaking continued, though diminishing quickly.

Seconds later, the quake stopped. All was dark. I whispered, "Sam, are you all right?"

She coughed. "I'm okay, except that you're stepping on my foot."

I slid my foot back. "Better?"

"Yep." A light shone in my eyes. "And the penlight still works."

I took it from her. As I straightened, dirt and pebbles slid down my shirt, now clinging to my damp back, moistened by blood and sweat. More pain sliced in, but I tried to ignore it as I swept the thin beam around.

The tunnel behind the transmitter had collapsed, blocking the passage. Above our heads, something stuffed the hole leading up to the room we had just left. That chamber had probably collapsed as well, sealing the exit.

"The quake didn't last long," Sam said. "You must have stopped it."

"I think you're right." I fastened Mastix to my belt. "But we're trapped."

"We can dig out, right?" Sam pushed a pile of debris back with her hands and feet. "This stuff moves pretty easily."

I pointed the beam at the tunnel blockade. "That stuff won't."

"I wish I had more of my super strength back. Then I could do it."

"Maybe, but I can't grant that wish. Not without my invention." I sat cross-legged on the clear spot we had made and let out a long sigh. "Mom used to say, if wishes were horses, beggars would ride."

Sam sat in front of me in the same pose. "Princess Queenie says if wishes were fishes, too many would flounder. But I never understood it."

I laughed in spite of the pain. "A flounder is a kind of fish, and it also means to move clumsily. She meant if you focus too much on wishes instead of reality, you'll lead a clumsy life. Actually, it's a pretty clever saying."

She blinked. "But what's all of that got to do with fishes?"

"Fishes rhymes with wishes. It's like a poem and the words …" I shook my head. "Never mind. We're getting off track."

Sam pouted, her face dim in the glow of the beam. "Well, I think she's wrong. I like to wish. It makes me feel better."

I let her words sink in. Sam so desperately wanted to feel better. And no wonder. Here we were in deep darkness with the threat of painful death literally hanging over our heads. Not only that, we didn't know if Mom was dead or alive. Maybe getting Sam to talk more would help. "What kinds of things do you wish for?"

Her eyes sparkled with tears as her voice pitched a notch higher. "I wish Daddy was alive. I wish Mommy would smile more. I wish we didn't always need money. And I wish we could get out of this horrid place."

"That's quite a list." I slid my hand into hers. "I can't do much about the first three, but we'll get out of here somehow. Just give me time to think."

After a few moments of silence, Sam sniffed. "Do *you* ever wish for anything?"

The penlight dimmed. I flicked it off to save the batteries. "Oh, I don't want to bother you with that."

"I'm your sister." She compressed my hand. "If you can't tell me, who can you tell?"

"I suppose you're right." I heaved another sigh. Just a couple of days ago, I couldn't have imagined spilling my feelings to her, but for some reason, now it seemed easy. "Well, I wish for the same stuff you said. If Dad were alive, things would be a lot better."

"Yeah." Her voice diminished to a whimpering whisper. "I miss him so much."

Her plaintive tone brought tears to my own eyes. "Me, too."

Gloom settled in, adding to the darkness. I had to cheer her up somehow. Cast off the gloom. "You know, I did get one of my biggest wishes. Maybe the biggest ever."

"What's that?"

"When Mom was pregnant with you, I wished for the coolest little sister possible."

"Really?" Her voice perked up. "You wanted a sister? Not a brother?"

"Really."

"Why?"

I shrugged, though she couldn't see my shoulders. "I thought maybe I would fight with a brother. Maybe a sister would be easier to get along with."

"We do fight. At least a little."

"Yeah. Sometimes. Not so much lately."

"And never again. I promise." After another moment of silence, she slid her arms around my neck and kissed my cheek. "I love you, Eddie."

"I love you, too, Sam." I ran a hand through her tangled hair and kissed her cheek in return. "We really are a good team."

She drew back. "The best. We saved Nirvana."

"Most likely. The quake was short."

"But now we need someone to save us."

The words *and Mom* came to mind. But no use adding to Sam's worries.

She shouted into the hole above us. "Help! We're trapped down here!"

Her voice bounced off the rocks and died.

"No one can hear us, Sam. And no one knows about the hole besides Mephisto. He won't tell anyone where we are."

"Then let's climb as far as we can and shout from up there."

"Sure. But let me rest for a few minutes. My back's killing me."

"All right." Silence ensued for the next few moments, except for Sam's fidgeting as she shifted debris around. Then a flashlight beam appeared. "Found it under some rocks," Sam said as she pointed it at me.

"Yeah, I left it here. And both remote controllers are buried somewhere."

She lifted my shirt, peeling it from my skin. "Ouchy. You're cut up pretty bad." She lowered my shirt back in place. "The blood's sticking."

"I know. So let's wait a few more —"

A rumble sounded from above. The ground shook, but not like a quake, more like vibrations from a passing truck.

As we rose together, I grabbed the light from Sam and aimed it up into the hole. A spinning drill, like a rotating unicorn's horn, tore through rocks and sent fragments raining on our heads.

"It's the magna-gopher." I unfastened Mastix, grasped Sam's hand, and backed away toward the tunnel blockade. The rumbles grew louder, and the vibrations shook the floor harder. The ceiling cracked and sent more debris over us.

Sam threw her arms around my waist. "Turnip Head's coming to finish us off."

I held Mastix in a ready position. The moment Mephisto's evil face appeared, he would get a lightning bolt right between the eyes.

The drill pushed into sight, then the vehicle, its front pointing downward. Shaped like the swamp tank, treads and all, the magna-gopher dropped to the floor and turned upright. It rumbled toward us, but with our backs against the blockade, we couldn't retreat any farther.

Just as I made ready to zap the gopher with Mastix, the rumbling machine halted, and the top hatch flung open. A man climbed out, stood upright on top, and banged his head on the chamber's low ceiling.

As he rubbed his scalp, I pointed the light at him, but he blocked it with an arm. "That light is glaring, garish, and …"

"Gilbert!" Sam shouted over the motor's noise.

I swung the beam away and shone it on myself so he could see us.

Gilbert lowered his arm and blinked. "Ah. Excellent. You're both alive." He reached into the gopher, shut off the engine, and climbed down to the floor. "Your mother will be most pleased at this happy turn of events."

"Great to see you." I put Mastix away and shook his hand. "How did you find us?"

"I followed the signal with my controller locator."

"You could follow it through all of that rock?"

"Not easily. The signal was quite weak. But a certain fellow came along who suggested that I dig through that hole I just came through. Worked like a charm."

"Fellow? What fellow?"

Gilbert blinked. "Middiken? Maddigan? …"

"Milligan?"

He pointed at me. "Masterfully remembered."

I whispered to myself. "That's right. Milligan *did* know about the hole."

"And it's a good thing he followed us to the Stellar building," Gilbert continued. "When Lamar was about to bury us with the gopher, Milligan accosted him with considerable skill and rendered him unconscious. It seems that Lamar was distracted by a radio conversation."

"Where's our mother?" Sam asked.

Gilbert pointed upward. "At street level with Milligan and Prince Edward. The short quake made the passage down here unsafe. Therefore, I must now ferry you to her. The cockpit is designed for only one, so even with a single extra passenger, it will be a tight squeeze."

I nodded. "Take Sam. I'll be fine down here till you get back."

"Of course. Ladies first."

After Gilbert reboarded, I helped Sam climb up and join him. The motor restarted with a rumble. Within a couple of minutes, they had climbed back up the hole and out of sight. When the noise died away, I turned off the flashlight and sat on a waist-high boulder.

In spite of the pains ripping across my body, I let myself smile. What a day it had been! We really did it. We saved Nirvana. Of course, we had a lot of rebuilding to do, but at least we had saved thousands upon thousands of lives. Maybe some of our wishes were finally coming true.

CHAPTER 24

Superheroes Sprouting All Over the Place

Several minutes later, the magna-gopher's engine noise returned. When Gilbert arrived and parked, I squeezed in with him and rode to the surface. The moment he opened the hatch, I climbed out on top of the vehicle and looked around.

Mom and Sam stood on the shattered street. Both waved at me, Sam carrying Prince Edward. At a nearby building, Milligan leaned against its cracked wall, his eyes averted.

I climbed down and wrapped one arm around Mom and the other around Sam. Our three-way hug felt so good. This crazy, dangerous adventure was finally over.

For the ride home, Sam and I sat atop the swamp tank while Mom and Gilbert rode inside with the top open. To the rear, Milligan followed on his motorcycle, almost out of sight. During the journey, I scanned the torn-up city and its downed power lines, broken pavement, and cracked buildings.

Some people were already climbing ladders and hammering boards over windows. Others poured concrete from wheelbarrows and patched cracks. A few waved at us as we passed. Two or three gave us curious stares, but no one bothered to ask about the odd tank beneath us.

While we rode, Mom filled Gilbert in on what she knew about our adventures, and I inserted a few details. Gilbert nodded from time to time and interjected with alliterating comments, making us all laugh.

Exhausted, I turned to Sam and petted Prince Edward as he sat curled in her lap. It would be so good to get home, get cleaned up and bandaged, and go to sleep. I could think about helping with restoring Nirvana later.

When we arrived at our building, Mom stayed behind in the lobby to talk with Milligan while Barney escorted Gilbert, Sam, and me to our apartment, telling us that it was one of the few safe units in the complex. He had restored electricity with his generator, and since we were the only residents who had returned so far, he gave us permission to turn on whatever electrical devices we wanted to use.

Once inside, Gilbert asked to use my computer, saying he wanted to see what kind of coded logic lay behind the Damocles AI program. While he worked at my desk and Sam watched, I gathered a few bottles of water and limped to the bathroom.

After washing from a basin, I walked stiff-legged to my bedroom, wearing loose-fitting pants and shirt to keep the material from sticking to my wounds. I carried my dirty, torn clothes over one arm and the gadgets belt over the other, Mastix still attached, and tossed everything on my bed.

At my desk, Gilbert stared at the computer

screen, seemingly unaware of my entry into the room. Sam bounced on her mattress, chanting the Princess Queenie song, her smile wide as she waved for me to join her. "Sing it with me."

I leaped onto the bed and sang along while bouncing. "Princess Queenie, fairy blessed, of all the fairies, you're the best. Spread your sparkles far and wide. Take me on a sparkle ride."

With a final bounce, she sailed into my arms. I hugged her close and spun with her, ignoring the pain. She was so worth it.

When we climbed down, I sat on my bed. Sam picked up Prince Edward and cuddled with him next to me. Around the room, cracks still ran along the walls, and holes marred the ceiling. Barney had a lot of work ahead of him.

His stare still locked on the computer monitor, Gilbert tapped on the keyboard. The original AI version of Damocles appeared on the screen, the dumb one who lacked his essence. Next to the AI window, programming code scrolled while Gilbert watched the lines pass by.

Mom walked in with a first-aid kit. While she medicated and bandaged my wounds, Sam chattered on and on about our adventures, though both Mom and Gilbert had already heard most of them. Sam's version, though, made me wonder how much the tales would grow. She already added a magic sparrow that whispered flying instructions as she flew over the swamp. Guardian fairies would probably be next.

When Mom applied the final bandage, I stood

and looked over Gilbert's shoulder. "What are you trying to find?"

"Actually, I already found it." He spun in the chair and faced us. "A way to create a new animated hologram of our dear, departed Damocles. You can use it as the face of your heroic efforts from now on, as it will be programmable, practical, and personal."

"So villains will still believe he's alive?"

"Precisely."

"That'll be great." I patted him on the back. "Thanks, Gilbert."

"But there is one curious item remaining. When I powered the computer up, this AI version of Damocles was about to say something, a personal message to you, so I stopped it until you were ready to listen."

"Should we leave the room?" Mom asked.

I shook my head. "Anything Damocles has to say to me, you guys can hear."

"Very well." Gilbert's finger hovered over a key. "When everyone's ready."

Mom and I closed in on the computer. Sam released Prince Edward and stood on my bed to look on.

Gilbert tapped the key. "Restarting."

Damocles walked toward the foreground until his face filled the screen. As his eyes shifted, the camera on top of the monitor rotated. "Eddie, Sam, two unrecognized adults, and one gray cat, I have a parting message. I scanned the news and learned that you succeeded in your quest to neutralize

Mephisto and save Nirvana. Congratulations on a job well done."

I gave him a nod, though he was just an AI unit. "Thanks."

"Do you have the wallet I gave you?"

"I think it's attached to the computer." I found it on the desk. The wallet's built-in cable led to the computer's port. Inside the wallet, the embedded disk was still covered and tightly sealed, as yet an unsolved mystery. "Yep. It's here."

Damocles looked straight at me. Although his lips didn't move, a voice emanated, no longer robotic. "I am the real Damocles. I recorded this message before I died. I hereby transfer my superhero mantle to you. Wear it well, with courage, humility, sacrifice, and above all, love. These are the true qualities of a superhero."

The wallet sizzled. The seal over the disk burned away, leaving behind a medal of gold attached to a leather cord. Smoke rose from fiery letters engraved on the surface. When the smoke cleared, I read the words out loud. "Superhero – Eddie Hertz (aka Archimedes)."

"It's real gold," the recording continued, "and it's for you. Good-bye, and may you be the greatest superhero the world has ever known."

The sound died away, and the screen blinked off.

Sam whispered, "Wow."

My hands shaking, I lifted the medal, draped the cord over my neck, and tied it in the back. As the disk swayed at my chest, the gold glimmered.

Mom and Gilbert both patted me on the shoulder.

"You deserve it," Mom said. "Your father would be so proud of you."

I turned to her. "You think so?"

"I know so." She kissed my forehead. "You're my superhero."

"Hooray for Eddie!" Sam bounced from my bed.

I caught her in midflight and spun her in a circle. "I couldn't have done it without you, squirt."

She grinned from ear to ear. "That's 'cause we're a team."

"You better believe it."

"Uh … excuse me?"

We all turned toward the voice. Barney stood at the bedroom doorway, Milligan pacing behind him. Barney pointed over his shoulder with a thumb. "This … er … gentleman says he's family. Is that true?"

Mom nodded. "Thank you, Barney. I was expecting him."

When Barney left, Milligan walked in and took off his baseball cap, revealing tangled hair matted with blood. A line of stitches ran along each cheek. His fight in the Dead Zone had taken quite a toll.

Mom looped an arm around his and faced us. "Eddie. Sam. Your Uncle Milligan wants to say something to you. Just remember, he saved our lives. Yours. Sam's. Gilbert's and mine. And he led us to find you and Sam."

I lowered Sam to the floor and held her hand, trying to keep my composure. The thought of his treachery stabbed me once again. "I understand. Let's hear what he has to say."

Milligan cleared his throat. "Yeah … well … Eddie. I've done a lot of bad things in the past, but I hope we can forget about all that and let bygones be bygones. I got a lot of connections, and I can help out here financially. You and your mom and Sam deserve a lot better than this hole you're living in. Maybe I can make up for my … well … I'll just come right out and say it. My crimes against your family. Our family."

I tried to read his eyes. Maybe I should believe him, and maybe I shouldn't. But if Mom could give him a second chance, so could I. "Sure, Uncle Milligan. It'll be great to have your help."

He blew out a relieved sigh. "Thanks, Eddie. I appreciate it."

Sam ran to him and threw her arms around his waist. "Welcome to our family."

He picked her up and held her at his hip with one arm. "I also have some news. That big guy I clubbed got away in a helicopter. After I told your mom where I thought she could find you, I spotted the chopper in the air and followed it on foot as far as I could. He picked up some other guy in the Dead Zone. By the time I got there, they were out of reach. The second guy wrote something, tied it to a weight, and dropped it."

Milligan withdrew an envelope from his pocket and handed it to me. From inside, I withdrew a small scrap of paper and read the neatly printed words out loud. "It's not over, Eddie. Ask Gilbert about the hypnotizing gas. Until next time. Mephisto."

Gilbert's eyes widened. "Oh, dear."

I showed him the paper. "What do you know about this?"

As he read it, he fidgeted in his seat. "I created such a gas to hypnotize my birds so I could do minor surgery when needed."

I slid the note back to the envelope and tossed it to the desk. "Damocles mentioned getting a hypnotic vision after being shot by a poison pellet. I guess that means it works on humans."

Gilbert nodded. "Quite well. I hypnotized myself once. I didn't come out of it for several hours."

"Can it be used on a large scale?"

"I'm afraid so. Under the right conditions, quite large. All of Nirvana, in fact."

I picked up my gadgets belt, strapped it on, and slid my hand around Mastix. The thongs glowed, ready to be whipped into action. "Then we'll just have to stop him again."

Sam wriggled down from Milligan and grasped my hand. "Together. We're a superhero team."

"Always together." I scanned the others in the room — Mom, Gilbert, Milligan, and a gray tabby named Prince Edward Thomas Oscar Stephen Horsey O'Ryan. Who could ask for a better team?

"Well, Sam," I said, "it looks like we have new candidates. Think they're ready to join us?"

She grinned. "Only if I'm allowed to give them superhero names."

"Perfect." I winked at her. "If they can remember their new names, then they're on the team."